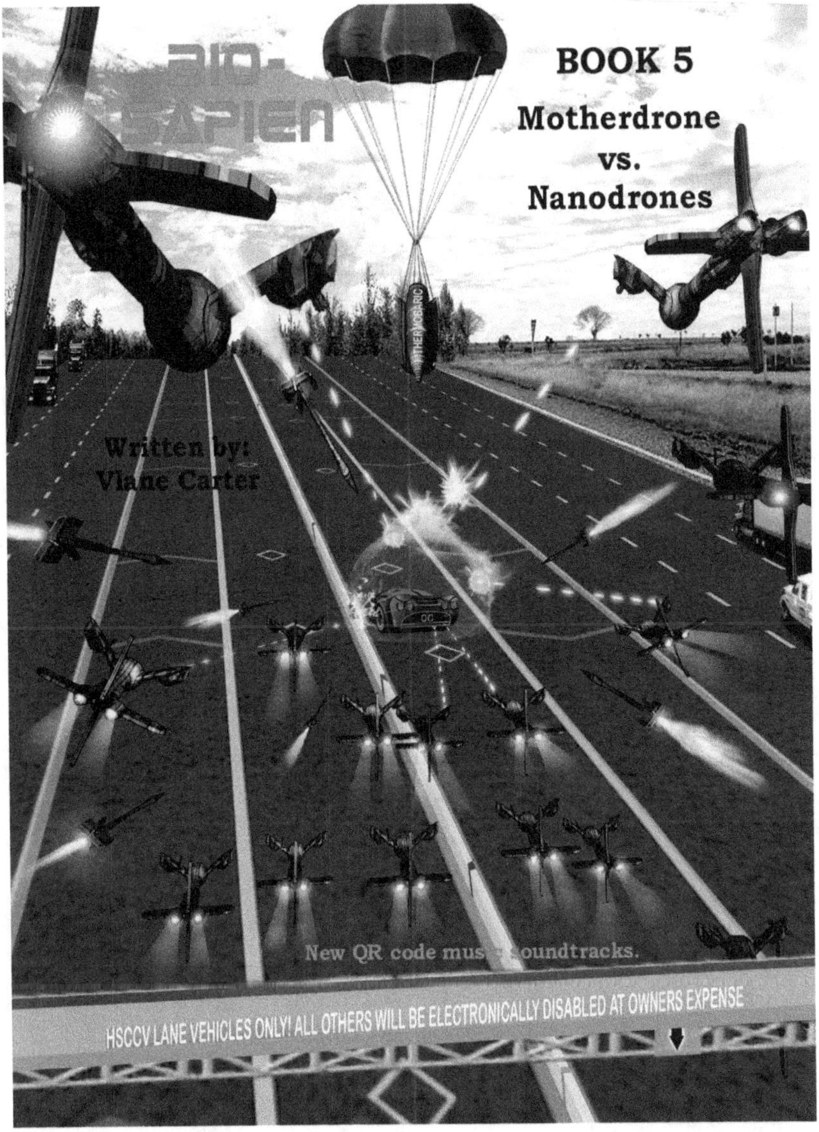

BIO-
SAPIEN

BOOK 5
Motherdrone
vs.
Nanodrones

Written by:
Vlane Carter

New QR code music soundtracks.

BIO-Sapien Comics & Novels.

Take a 360 video tour of Action Burger:

Action Burger's latest music video on youtube:

BIO-SAPIEN 101

JADEN'S HUMAN BODY BIO-ENGINEERED WITH ALIEN NANOTECHNOLOGY.

CONTROL YOUR BODY LIKE A STAR TREK ENTERPRISE SHIP.
CAPTAIN OF BIO-SAPIEN HOST: Jaden Marino. 5'10-6'1 155LBS.
SECOND OFFICER IN CHARGE: AI – (AISCAN) Artificial Intelligent Synthetic Crystal Andromedian Nanobot.

CREW MEMBERS: NANODRONES (+1000 Quintillion) PCBOALF
– Prototype Carbon and Biochemical-based Organic Alien Life Forms; Also known as organic Nanobots.

LEFT ARM
– Atom Ripper Nanodrones embedded in skin, based on plasma fusion technology.

SPINAL CORD AND BACK
– Energy shield generating Nanodrones storage area. Brain controls RPM speed and direction of energy shield outside of body. Energy shield is base on plasma fusion technology and Neutrino energy. It retrieves most of its energy from replaced digestive system area.
– Magnetically charged Nanodrones enhances intervertebral disc of cartilage.

SKELETON
– Reconstructed Cancellous and Compact bones. Nanodrone webs of organic fiber proteins. 500 pounds per square inch of force needed to break a bone.

JOINTS
– Enhanced synovial joints around body. Magnetic energy between Nanodrones in joints makes the joints 10x stronger and flexible.

PENIS
– Multiple joints added to penal shaft for controllable directional curving.

COPYRIGHT 2010 BY: VU IMAGINATION FACTORY
Illustration by: John Moriarty
Creative art director: Vlane Carter

BRAIN
– Rostral anterior cingulate cortex – Unknown signals transmitted when host feels pain or becomes angry.
– Instant on internal forward moving one layer energy shield, that extends around the skull.

EARS
– Enhanced equilibrium in inner ears. Nanodrones in ears communicate hi-speed with pro-gravity and magnetic Nanodrones in feet. They also communicate with anti-gravity Nanodrones in kidney/lower spine. Allows host to walk on walls or ceilings and feel as if he is walking on the ground.

ARMS
– Specially modified cells and tissue to accept high-energy forces.

RIGHT ARM
– Gravity shockwave Nanodrones embedded in skin.

MUSCLES
– Myostatin protein in muscles cells modified. MSTN gene decoded.
– On demand muscle strength equivalent to 2-4HP.
– Musculoskeletal - Nanodrones enhances muscle fibers strength and coordinate with skeleton system.

RIGHT KIDNEY
– Internal tissue removed. Nanodrones doing the same job in the blood around body. Kidney replaced with quadrillions of Anti-gravity Nanodrones.

NERVOUS SYSTEM
– Nanodrones in brain bypasses chemical messages during Nanotime. They transmit hi-speed collective signals at 8000 feet per second to Nanodrones at nerve endings.

FEET
– Pro-gravity and magnetic Nanodrones; works directly with equilibrium in ears.

LEGS
– Enhanced muscles enables host to run and average between 20-30Mph.
– Host can jump an unlimited height with anti-gravity Nanodrones support.

BIO-SAPIEN 101

JADEN'S HUMAN BODY BIO-ENGINEERED WITH ALIEN NANOTECHNOLOGY.

CAPTAIN OF BIALIEN HOST: Jaden Marino.

SECOND OFFICER IN CHARGE: AI (AISCAN) Artificial Intelligent Synthetic Crystal Andromedian Nanobot.

ALIEN NANOTECHNOLOGY:

NANODRONES (+1000 Quintillion) PCBOALF – Prototype Carbon and Biochemical-based Organic Alien Life Forms. Also known as organic Nanobots. - Varies in size.
- Communicate in an atomic digital level 3 collective.
- Split into trillions of communities to perform millions of different duties in organic host.
- Nanodrones are loyal to the DNA of one host.

BRAIN
- 200 billion enhanced neurons.
- Neural code decoded. Neurotransmitters enhanced.
- New multitasking matrix area in the brain.
- RPM control area for forward and reverse energy shields.
- Artificial nicotine cigarette stimulation. Reconfigured Dopamine areas of the brain.
- Total brain usage 60-100%: up from 7-10% average Homosapien.
- Nanotime accelerates the communication speed in the brain. Time dilation reroutes to different parts of the brain. Nanodrones create artificial neurons, artificial synapses and axons. Host witnesses everything happening outside the body in slow motion. Nanotime ranges from 1x to 100x. 1x is the slowest speed and host can see a bullet approaching. Negative side is Nanotime puts a strain on brain and lasts only seconds; can lead to seizures.

LUNGS
Nanodrones double lung capabilities. 30% more carbon dioxide leaves lungs from added oxygen breathing Nanodrones in skin.
- Instant on internal forward moving one layer energy shield, that extends through the rib cage and around heart.

DNA
10,000 compressed DNA memo groups in various locations around body.
- Encoded DNA. Built in anti-cloning prevention. DNA strips away when it leaves host.
- Modified DNA and RNA genetic code.
- Advanced protein folding.

BLOOD
- Reprogrammed white and red blood cells to accept Nanodrones.
- Artificial stem cells regeneration capacities. Rapid injury repair system.

- Turn the human host into a powerful offensive and defensive weapon.

Enhanced rods and cones behind eyes. 1 terapixels of resolution in each eye.
- Jaden's eyes command screen. Nanodrones reports; body's actions, offense and defense weapons, energy updates, statistics, energy shield RPM and navigation info.
- Nanoscanner images transmit to optic-nerve.

They pass through and scan any matter. They transmit sound, smell, vision and taste to host. They can also carry trillions of Nanodrones to do remote tasks. Nanoscanners also help to return gravity shockwave and atom ripper Nanodrones back to host.

- Artificial orbital hybridization web binds with skin cells; also known as Nanodrone nanotubing organic fibers.

- Self cleaning skin - Bacteria and dirt deposits around body pulls into skin and manually transported securely in blood stream by skin.

- Advanced photosynthesis in skin. Sunlight provides carbohydrate energy into blood stream. Host does not have to eat for days.

- 100% filtered oxygen absorbed through pores and injected into the blood stream. Host can hold breathe for 20-30 minutes. 30% carbon dioxide leaves Nanodrones can also reproduce air temperature to match body heat.

- Light reflecting Metamaterial Nanodrones embedded around skin.

STOMACH, SMALL, AND LARGE INTESTINES
- Unnecessary organs; removed. Replaced with: Nanodrones energy storage areas. Atomic Solar Recharge fusion area and sub-atomic particles smashing areas.
- Nanodrones protect every, outer cell in area from radiation energies.
- Nanodrones can do the same ob the digestive system does in a fraction of an inch. Vitamins, minerals, salts, water, carbohydrates, amino acids from proteins, H2O, and fats from food, filter in seconds directly into the blood stream from the throat area. The rest redirects into the buttocks area for storage.
- Nanodrones redirect and duplicate chemical messages to let the brain know the organs are still there.

NANODRONE GOALS
- Remove and replace unnecessary body parts/organs.
- Evolve the BIO body to its maximum capabilities.
- Avoid alien metamorphosis : Defend and protect host.
- De-frag and recalibrate the brain configuration for ultimate performance.
- Avoid technological singularity.

EYES
Nanodrones reports; body's actions, offense and zooming capabilities.

NANOSCANNERS
(Six Nanoscanners created from Nanodrones made for BIO host).
Autonomous alien molecules that vary in size.

SKIN
Skin will evolve to be stronger than Kevlar.
Nanodrones to throat area.
Nanodrones can produce oxygen. When combined with water can produce oxygen.
hair follicles on head.
signature.

WWW.BIO-SAPIEN.COM

5

BIO-SAPIEN VOLUME I (BOOKS 1-6).

PROLOGUE

An average teenager Jaden Marino discovers a UFO landing one evening in upstate NY. The government is also looking for the mysterious UFO in the area. The government eventually follows him to it while trying to kill him. He hides inside of the advanced nanotechnology UFO while the government tries to take it away to Area 51 on a trailer. His mind goes into a comatose state and he has an out-of-the-body experience. The spaceship translates his English language from his mind into its language, enabling him to control the UFO with his mind. As he tries to fly away, the government sends all of their best and top-secret aircraft to intercept this very advanced spacecraft. Jaden quickly learns what this spaceship is capable of and goes against the best pilots in an intense chase over NY. Eventually he leaves Earth and travels 2.1 million light-years into the Andromeda Galaxy. He learns of an advanced alien species called Andromedians, who are 70,000 years ahead of humans. The Andromedians are peaceful explorers and their thinking is very far ahead of our own.

Jaden comes back to Earth eighteen years later and is aware of an alien conspiracy that is about to take place on Earth. He tries to warn people, but everyone thinks he is crazy. They lock him up in a mental ward. Society, relationships, values and technology has changed on Earth. He has a microscopic artificial intelligence alien companion in his mind helping him along the way, called AI. His body begins developing its advanced alien nanotechnology weapons system to work on Earth. After the government and citizens do not listen, he tries to help the people he cares about while the government places him on a terrorist list and uses their full military forces to kill him. He goes against the government's future weapons, Motherdrone (a super computer that controls all UAV drone crafts), super exoskeleton soldiers, SWATbots, thermobaric weapons and himself. At the same time, a bad alien race, called Darclonians, are implementing their silent planned strike on humans. An energy knight is the Darclonians new powerful weapon that can manipulate dark energy. Unbelievable movie style action sequences throughout the book and an ending you won't stop talking about. Jaden Marino's adventure of a lifetime begins.

BIO-SAPIEN SERIES (Formally known as the BiAlien trilogy.)

VOL I PROFESSIONAL BOOK REVIEWS

NOTE: Book reviews are based on all six books to volume I series.

"Science fiction fans unite! If the title doesn't say it all, I don't know what will! To preface this review, all of you naysayers out there who shake their heads at sci-fi should remember that, back in the 70's, the names R2-D2, C3PO, Chewie...you get my point, here...were unknowns. Now they are as much a facet of popular literary culture as is Mr. Darcy. Jane Austen, Henry James, Dickens, etc., were beautiful storytellers, but sci-fi has amazingly imaginative beauty surrounding it as well. And this author, Vlane Carter, knows that for a fact....

...there are A LOT of scenes that the reader gets to experience. From the military battle with the UFO, to the alien shark attack on another planet (which is really cool, by the way), this author offers a never-ending parade of amazing creatures and locations that will, perhaps, one day be logged into popular literary culture right beside old C3PO and his little beeping buddy......

There are two factions out there in America - Star Wars vs. Star Trek - and I am definitely on the side of George Lucas having the more creative concept. So hats off to this writer, Vlane Carter, who may someday join those Lucas ranks if readers and sci-fi fans everywhere band together and realize that the force really MAY be with this one." – **FEATHERED QUILL REVIEWS.**

"....the bialien trilogy is not your typical sci-fi novel. Think of a comic book that uses words instead of illustrations and you might come close. One thing that the writer certainly has is imagination. It is written very visually....

.....you may tell by his style that Vlane is very passionate about his writing. It takes time and effort to envision and write a novel of this length without losing the energy throughout it.

Bialien is his first novel, and, from his marketing material and website, certainly not his last. It is always interesting to see the first story written and how writing styles evolve from book to book. Let's see where Volume Two takes us." –**TOP BOOK REVIEWERS.**

"A Sci-Fi series set on exploring concepts of the deep future, "The Bialien Trilogy" is for the Science fiction fan who likes to be amazed at what the future holds...." - MIDWEST BOOK REVIEWS

"Vlane Carter first novel is a huge "tome" of a book. There is lots of action and adventure as our main character, Jaden, meets a host of aliens from across the universe, engages in a host of battles as well as doing some "fun" stuff. There is a lot of "things" in this book to cause the reader to pause and ponder. For the adventurous reader who likes long novels make sure you put this close to the top of your Must Read list.—**STEVEN FIVECATS, EDITOR. YELLOW30 SCI-FI REVIEW.**

"...the first thing readers will notice about this book is the author's manner of storytelling. It's different and can take some getting use to. That said, if you adjust your thinking to the author's way of telling the story, you'll find that it works! He achieves his goal of making the story read as if you're seeing it on the big screen, as an action packed movie. Also worth mentioning, is that to complete the entire scope of the story, Vlane has placed visual images throughout, as well as a book sound track, creating an entirely new dimension to the meaning of author/story/reader interaction....

....Outside of the book itself, this author takes great care to interact with his readers and has a website that includes free chapter plus loads of information about the series. Inside the book, he takes just as much care, and it's clear he has put his entire being into each and every word. Real knowledge can make or break a book, and this author definitely knows his technology. ....

....Give this book a chance and you won't be disappointed by the in your face, non-stop action that leaves you on a roller coaster ride that thrusts you up and down, side to side, both thrills and chills, and then rockets you out of this world..."
-New Reads Underground. Rachel M. D'aigle, NRU Head and Author of YA Fantasy Series The Journals of The Jacoby Odyssey

---

....This book crosses many topics, from government conspiracies, alien technology, nanotechnology, world domination, love, female empowerment and religion... All which take the reader into new realms of thought and possibility, allowing for outside the box thinking and discussion amongst readers.....

....Sci-fi and fiction enthusiasts will have a hard time putting this book down. Vlane Carter succeeds in his unconventional storytelling style, drawing readers into his vast creation, while the plot twists keep you riveted and guessing until the books final page. Or, make that the final word...." **-M. Penny Harmon, Review SIP "ReviewSIP" (Salt Lake City, Utah)**

TO ALL READERS AND BOOK CRITICS PLEASE NOTE:

BIO-Sapien was written in present tense for the following reasons:

1. So the reader can read and experience the novel as if they were watching a movie.
2. Nanotime.
3. Detailed action sequences.
4. Movie soundtracks inserted into different parts of the story.
5. Telepathic communication and talking to another personality.
6. Mind reading and answering questions inside of a conversation.
7. Have the reader experience the story as if they are right with Jaden at all times.

"....Author, Vlane Carter, has created a story told in a unique and unconventional writing style, keeping the action in the present tense, so as to keep the reader feeling as though they are experiencing the action as its happening. It can be akin to reading a script, or make you feel as though you're watching a movie. It is a writing style that can, at first, be jarring and difficult to understand. But if you give it a few chapters it will not only grow on you, but draw you in. And then you suddenly cannot imagine the story written any other way. And, quite possibly, it could be the first book that includes its own music recommendations (to listen to while reading)....." - M. Penny Harmon, Review SIP "ReviewSIP"

Single quotes ' ' are used in the book when:

To show main character Jaden communicating with his alien friend AI (located in his mind).
High-speed telepathic communications.

What happened in BIO-Sapien books 3 & 4?

Book 3 starts off with Jaden returning to Earth in his upgraded EIS, eighteen years later by earth time.

His bio-engineered body is slowly evolving into superhuman levels. His mission is to help scientist locate the Nanomole in humans and then deactivate it, before the Darclonian mothership enters broadcast range. When a Nanomole is activated and is in the correct stage, it can control a human body. It would need to synchronize with a Bio-parasite for a permanent takeover of the human mind (Bio-parasites are Darclonians in microbe form).
There is the first female president on television, along with commercials on holographic discs, 3D televisions, electric cars and online Third Virtual life. There are also doctors in robotic remote controlled LCD screens.

Times have changed and societal values have deteriorated significantly with the advent of the technology age. The combination of cheating, negotiated infidelity, high divorce rates, male and female robotic companions, and online virtual sex have helped to erode fundamental human values.

Jaden is aware of an silent alien attack that is about to take place against humans. A countdown will soon begin, ending with all human brains being highjacked by Nanomoles. Nanomoles are Darclonian microbes deposited on Earth after the last ice age. When the mother ship gets close enough to Earth, they activate and an eighty-four hour countdown begins.

Jaden tries to warn people, but everyone thinks he is crazy. They lock Jaden up in a psychiatric ward until they find out who he is, since his DNA doesn't show up on any scans and he doesn't remember who he is. A doctor uses an experimental FMRI (digital simulacrum of the neocortex) machine on Jaden to find out who he is and where he has been. This machine scans and translates chemical messages into digital images. His Nanodrones are up for their first challenge. In the meantime, the US government received a space message from the Andromedians, but didn't take the threat seriously.

In the area of Jaden's mind that governs different personalities, there is a microscopic artificial intelligence alien companion named AI. Specifically designed for his mission on Earth, AI helps Jaden navigate his upgraded mind and body, and is second in charge of the colony of Nanodrones throughout Jaden's body. Jaden and AI slowly develop a relationship as they learn from each other. Jaden teaches AI how to think non-linearly and how to become more human, while AI teaches Jaden how to multi-task and use his evolved body. AI has to figure out a way to develop Jaden's super human powers to work around Earth's natural properties so they can break out of the mental hospital before the government finds him. In order for this to happen, AI needs Internet access so he can download terabytes of science and technology information. AI then runs high-speed experiments with the Nanodrones and removes Jaden's unnecessary organs for energy and weapons storage.

Some of Jaden's super human powers include defying gravity, nanoscanners, controlling gravity in a weapon called a gravity shockwave, molecule ripper, reflecting light, creating two advanced energy shields around plasma fusion technology and accelerating his body to react in milliseconds. The alien nanotechnology in his body replaces vital organs such as the stomach, liver, small and large intestines, to make room for his offense and defense systems.

Jaden meets Dr. Chan, a Forensic Scientist. She is at the psychiatric ward to investigate why his DNA can't be identified. She first believes he is crazy and is not revealing his true identity. Jaden agrees to "show" her the truth instead of telling her.
His Nanodrones transmit his memories through his hand into her brain. While he is showing her who he is and where he has been, Jaden unlocks and reads her nanomole that holds her family history and genetic memories for thousands of years. Nanomoles record humans' five senses, emotions, memories, experiences and personalities. Jaden is able to experience what Dr. Chan's grandmother experienced as a child during the China Nanking Massacre in 1937.

Dr. Chan and Jaden both exchange memories and they develop a familiarity with each other in ten minutes that would normally take two people twenty years.

It is a race against time when Jaden's old government nemesis Vice President Robinson finds out he has returned to Earth. Robinson puts Jaden on a terrorist list and uses all the government's resources to kill him. While Jaden tries to escape from the hospital, someone gets in his way. He has his first fight against a hospital security guard in an exoskeleton bionic suit.

Jaden later changes his identity by changing his facial structure and pigmentation in order to board an airplane to North Carolina to find his father. At higher altitudes, some Nanomoles go into the second stage. A passenger has an unstable nanomole in his brain, freaks out and opens the emergency exit at 33,000 feet. The man falls out, taking with him the air marshal who tried to stop him. While the 737 bails to lose altitude, Jaden runs towards the emergency exit and jumps after the two men without a parachute.

Jaden sees what his evolved body is capable of as he is determined to rescue the falling men. Later, the same aircraft is flying on autopilot while all the passengers and crew members are unconscious from their Nanomoles being in stage two. The government orders the plane shot down for fear that Jaden the terrorist took over. From a state away, Jaden, AI, Nanodrones and nanoscanners work together to remote into the pilot's brain to control him like a puppet.

In the next chapter, Jaden gets help from some close friends in an attempt to help the people he cares about. More and more humans are in deep sleeps, while some are walking around like zombies as their Nanomoles interact with chemical messages in the brain.

Vice President Robinson keeps President S. Paylin in complete ignorance on the impending alien attack. Robinson believes Jaden is the conspirator and is causing the strange disorders in humans. Robinson begins his own conspiracy to be the next president of the United States.

As the story develops, Jaden realizes something is happening to him. Something unknown is deep inside of him and he rides the line between good and evil. He finds himself thinking of evil things when he feels pain or becomes angry. Unknown dark energy forms around his hands and fingers. This energy slowly destroys Jaden's skin, but the energy also seriously affects AI's systems in Jaden's brain.

The plot continues when local police arrest Jaden and he begins to lose hope in trying to save humanity. Jaden decides to save his family and close friends instead of all humans.

Dr. Chan and Jaden have a unique physical connection in the previous chapter. BIO-Sapien volume I book 5 starts now.

BIO-Sapien book 5 – Nanodrones vs Motherdrone

Chapter 22: Full Throttle 1204 hp Car Chase

THE YEAR 2019 BUGATTEE SPORTS CAR - 1st GENERATION MARS SERIES

The Bugattee is a futuristic concept (green technology) sports car used in the BIO-sapien book 5.

Illustration by: John Buurman www.scifi-artpage.com
Creative art director and design by: Vlane Carter

Read more on this 2.4 million dollar sports car at:
WWW.BIO-SAPIEN.COM

SPECIFICATIONS:

Four independent wheel motor hybrid electric engines. Each 301 horsepower bi-cylinder hypercharged engine combines 5,319 pound-feet of total torque. Electrical color changing paint. 0-62mph in 2.11 seconds on Earth and a top speed of 301+mph

Four nanotube synthetic rubber nitrogen injection run flat Bad Year tires. Instant violation traffic system.

GREEN TECHNOLOGY: Hydrogen gas and electrical turbine grid system = 200 miles per gallon. Energy producing technologies: Advanced air vacuum filter system, solar cells, advanced electro-nanomaterial polymer battery system, mini air intake turbines, advanced hydraulic shocks, turbine spinning rims, kinetic energy brakes and two rear windmill turbine blades.

17

Chapter 22: Full throttle Car Chase @ 1204HP

Kimberly and Jaden sit on the side of a dirt road about seventy-five feet from her father's house.

"That is a nice mansion your father has," Jaden says.

"Thanks. What do you see?"

"There are two federal agents outside of your father's property using thermal vision machines. There is also a small UAV airplane flying in circles around his house. There is an army sniper about a hundred yards behind the house," he says.

"I wonder where my father is." She asks.

"I didn't sense anyone in the house. What are those spinning things on the roof of your father's house?" He asks.

"Those are jellyfish wind turbines. They spin around when the wind blows and create electricity for the entire house," she says.

"Cool, can't beat free electricity from Mother Nature," Jaden says.

'The Nanodrones are doing the same thing for your body now,' AI adds.

"I think we should sneak in through the side of the house," she says.

'The entrances have trap sensors in the doors and garage,' AI says.

"I think we should go in through a second floor window, there are traps in the doors and garage," Jaden says.

"How are we going to get up there?"

"I'll carry you up there. Are there any windows open?" He asks.

"Yes, the small bathroom window on the second floor is slightly open," she says.

'I have an idea, I can try to stimulate or trick the Nanomoles in the federal agents and sniper's brain to go into neutral mode,' AI says.

'Can you really do that?' Jaden asks.

'Yes, I just need to fill the nanoscanners up with Nanodrones and I think I can pull it off.'

'Cool, how long will it take?'

'It might take some time to mimic the mother ship's virtual proton transmissions. Maybe up to ten minutes, depending on the nanomole,' AI says.

"Jaden?" Kim asks.

'Get at it, good idea AI. It feels good being creative right?'

'Yes sir, it is as if I'm learning another culture and creating a non-linear idea,' AI says.

"Yes sweetie?" Jaden asks.

"I was just telling you about the second floor bathroom window and you zoned out on me," she says.

"Sorry, I was communicating with AI, he came up with an idea to put the three officers' Nanomoles into neutral, by mimicking the mother ship's signals."

"Cool. My plan is that I can climb through the small bathroom window then run around and open the bedroom window."

"That sounds good, but, sweetie, there isn't anyone in your house, but there is a human silicon faced robot lying in a bed upstairs. Made in Japan? Second generation? What is that thing? I almost thought it was a real man."

"That is my R.M.E.C. friend. I'll introduce you to him when we get inside. Are you ready?"

"Yes."

They leave the black SUV and Jaden gives Kimberly a piggyback ride. They quickly go invisible and he crosses a dirt road. They walk through some bushes. The UAV aircraft is still flying in circles high above the house.

'Jaden, that robot has a silicon penis under his pants and in its body.'

Jaden quickly switches his view through the nanoscanner to see for himself.

'Okay, this is getting weird. This robot has hair, fingers, skin, eyes, an ass, muscles and looks like a human man.'

'The nanoscanners are still working on the men; I think it will work,' AI says.

Jaden walks to the back of the small mansion. He bends his legs, "Hold on tight sweetie."

"Okay," she says as Jaden leaps fifteen feet to a small landing area outside the slightly open bathroom window. There are two more full size windows to the left, which are locked. She slowly pulls up the small bathroom window. The jellyfish turbines are quietly rotating above them.

"Do it very slowly, there is a sniper watching the back of the house," Jaden whispers.

'It worked, the two federal agents are unconscious.'

"Okay, I have to pee really bad baby," she says while climbing through the small window and standing on the floor. She pulls up her skirt and lowers her panties.

"Okay, but stay directly in front of me. So I can continue to block your body heat," Jaden says while Kimberly sits on the toilet near the window.

"Enjoying the view from above?" She asks.

"Yes I am, the view from any angle looking at you is enjoyable," he replies.

"That was a sweet thing to say," she says while flushing the toilet.

"The two federal agents are unconscious…"

"Great, I'll go open the hallway window for you," she says while jogging away.

"Kimberly! Kimberly! Come back!" Jaden yells in a loud whisper.

'The sniper sees her body heat. I'm not finished yet, this nanomole is not activating,' AI says.

'Shit, shit... hurry up. Can I create a shield around the window area?'

'The sensors in the doors downstairs and the UAV plane above can detect electromagnetic energy. They might fire another missile and blow up the mansion. Also, the shield might damage some of the house,' AI says.

Kimberly walks towards the hallway window and there is a red dot on her head.

'Shit, shit, shit, there is a red dot on her head,' Jaden says.

He quickly walks across the landing to the hallway window. The bullet is shot from 300 feet away and traveling at 3500 mph. Kimberly is smiling with a red dot in the middle of her head, while reaching for the window lock. Jaden puts his two hands together and slowly raises them. The invisible light reflecting Nanodrones reflects the infrared dot onto Kimberly's head.

"Arrrgggghhhh!" Jaden yells in a loud whisper.

Kimberly opens the window and sees blood dripping on the glass.

'Got him, the sniper is now unconscious,' AI says.

"You there baby? I don't see you. Is this your blood on the window?" She asks while Jaden becomes visible again.

He climbs through the window and stands on the floor.

"What happened to your hands baby?"

"I just took a bullet for you. The sniper had a red dot in the middle of your head," he says.

"Red dot? You said you took out the federal agents," she says.

"AI took out the two agents, but there was still an army sniper in the woods behind your father's house. You just ran off to open the hallway window," he says while showing her the bullet lodged between the palms of his hands.

"Oh my god, that bullet is stuck between your two hands. Are you okay?" She asks.

"I put my hands over the laser beam pointing towards your head and I stopped this 3500 mph bullet. This bullet would have splattered your brain all over the hallway and then it would have gone through the wall behind you. You have to be careful baby and listen more," Jaden says while pulling his hands apart and pulling out the bullet. The Nanodrones disinfect his wound.

'Your new skin is sixty percent finished regenerating,' AI says.

'I see. I thought I would have felt more pain,' he says.

Blood is going back into the wound from his hand. The bullet falls on the floor as a clear seal goes around the wound to keep the blood in. Nanodrones begin repairing his tissue, bones and muscle.

"I'm sorry sweetie. Thanks for taking that bullet for me," she says while picking up the bullet. She quickly drops it.

"That's still hot," she says in a surprised voice.

Suddenly, something approaches from behind them.

"Kimberly how are you today? You returned," the R.M.E.C. says with a human sounding male voice, while walking towards Kim.

She gives it a hug, while Jaden stands back and observes.

"I missed you today. You have been gone for over twenty-four hours. I am glad to see you are okay. I have cleaned the entire house twice. Should I prepare a meal at this house or your house?" The R.M.E.C. asks.

"Max, this is…this is…" she says while looking at Jaden, "Max this is my new boyfriend Jaden."

There is fifteen seconds of silence as Max looks at Jaden.

"Boyfriend? A favored male companion or sweetheart? A male friend in a romantic and sexual way?" Max asks while reaching his hand out to Jaden. He looks the robot in the face and they exchange handshakes.

"Nice to meet you, Mr. Max. That is a strong handshake you have there."

"Nice to meet you also sir."

'AI look at that, he can be your new friend.'

'I wonder if I can control him,' AI says.

22

'Don't think about it. You don't want to mess up her *male companion*,' Jaden says while chuckling.

'I'm sensing Max is jealous of you,' AI suggests.

'That is impossible. A robot can't be jealous. You can't be jealous right?'

'No, but as artificial intelligence robotics evolve they can be jealous just like humans. I have nothing to be jealous of. That is a mostly a human emotion.'

'Interesting. How long will the nanoscanners keep the soldier and agents asleep for?'

'Maybe twenty minutes, the scanners are reproducing the same signal the mother ship does.'

"Yes Max, that is who he is now, my boyfriend. You don't have to cook dinner tonight, we aren't staying too long. Do you know where my father went?" She asks while she walks to her bedroom and Jaden follows last. He smells the fresh fruity air fresheners in the air.

"He left with his lawyer to visit a local courthouse to find information about what happened to you. I overheard him saying you were in jail or prison. I've tried his cell phone several times, but it goes to voice mail," Max says.

Jaden follows Kim and Max around a corner into her bedroom. The huge room is light pink with flowers on the wall. She has Beyonce, Michelle Branch and Robin Thicke posters on the wall. Jaden realizes this must be her old room. The smell of different perfumes is in the air. Jaden sees Jennifer Lopez perfume and Narcissist body spray on her dresser. She looks in her dresser for some clothes. She takes off her skirt and blouse. Jaden and Max both look at her body.

"No, I wasn't in prison. Remember what I told you about eavesdropping?"

"Yes Kim," Max replies.

'Why is Max watching Kim undress also?' AI asks.

'I don't know, but this is very interesting.'

"Can I have some privacy?" She asks while they both are staring at her naked.

"Oh I'm sorry," Jaden says while turning around.

"Max can you run my shower and put these clothes in the bathroom. Then can you wait downstairs and try my father's cell phone some more."

"Yes Kim," Max says while walking away.

"Wow, he walks like the Terminator. His head goes first in the direction he wants to walk. That R.M.E.C. must have been expensive as hell. He looks like a real man. Now what is the deal with you two?" Jaden asks.

"Nothing, he is my male companion friend," she says while wrapping a towel around her body.

"That robot was jealous and he was looking at you naked," Jaden says.

She doesn't respond and passes Jaden, while walking in slippers. Jaden follows her into the main bathroom. She climbs into the shower and the water is already running. Jaden stands outside and waits for an answer. There is a yellow Jacuzzi on the other side of the bathroom.

"He was checking to see if I had any marks on me, he knows about my ex-boyfriend. He is my protector and friend. Do you want to shower also?" She asks.

"Come on, he was looking at your body like a man. I know what I saw. About the shower, my body self cleans itself…" he pauses and spits something brown into the toilet, "but I can shower anyway," Jaden says while taking off his clothes and climbing in.

The octagon-shaped shower is about five feet in diameter. The hot steaming water hits Jaden's body and makes him feel so good. He watches Kimberly wash herself with soap and water. She turns around and Jaden automatically washes her back.

"That feels good sweetie, you have nice hands," she says.

'The water against both of your bodies is hypnotizing' AI says.

24

"I have a cousin that visits from Taiwan sometimes and stays in the room down the hall, he is about your size. You can wear some of his clothes and get out of those clothes with bullet holes in them," she says while washing Jaden's back with soap.

'Max is down the hallway and walking up slowly to the bathroom door,' AI says.

"Quickie in the shower?" Jaden asks.

"No, baby I'm sore, you wore me out."

"What is the real deal with you and Max. I can tell he is a little jealous and why does he have a silicon dildo between his legs?" Jaden asks while washing himself.

There is silence as Kimberly's back is turned towards him and she continues to wash the lower parts of her body.

"I know you tried that bionic dildo, Kim. That is why you said earlier, you *missed* the real thing," Jaden says.

"Shouldn't you already know all of this?" She asks.

"No, when I was at the hospital downloading your memory into mine it didn't download the last two years. I was starting to deactivate your nanomole, but I didn't finish. That was when Ruffo came in, remember?" He asks.

There is still silence as the hot water rains down from the showerhead and steam continues to fill the huge bathroom.

"We don't have to talk about it if you don't want to," he says.

"No, I'll tell you...." she says but Jaden interrupts.

"Wait a second, what is this memory I'm seeing of you back in 2012 in college?"

"What memory do you mean?"

"What kind of crap do you college students watch on the Internet in your dorms? I'm going to be sick," he says while holding his mouth.

Jaden exits the shower and runs to the toilet dripping wet. He bends down, puts his head down into the toilet and throws up. Kim exits the shower and runs behind him.

"Jaden, what's wrong?"

25

He spits and gags into the toilet. He lifts his head out of the toilet and says, "Two girls and a cup? What the hell is wrong with you young people in the future? Have you lost your *Homo sapien* mind?" He asks while coughing.

"Oh that. Well I was caught off guard with that, my roommate had the webcam on videotaping my expression and then uploaded it into Myfacebook page. Sorry about that."

"That is NASTY! Where is God in those two girls' lives?" Jaden asks.

"It was nasty at the time, but people do that in *Third Virtual Life* all the time now. Some men like beautiful women doing that in a virtual environment. It's very disturbing," she says while drying herself off.

"Yes it is disturbing, don't worry about it, I'm erasing that memory from my memory. In a few seconds I'll forget all about it."

Jaden stands up and dries off with a Mr. LOL children's towel.

"Stop going through every personal memory of mine. Listen, I'll tell you the story about how I found more than a companionship with Max. Let me get this off my chest to you. As you know, my ex-boyfriends in the past broke my heart and cheated on me. I have always been in my books all my life. My father shielded me all my life from men and wanted me to do well in school first. When I finally graduated with my master's degree, I began dating men. I was very naïve at first and believed anything a man told me. I wanted to be a virgin until I got married, but my first boyfriend tricked me…" she says while drying off her hair.

"…and I lost my virginity to a man that didn't even love me back. He left me a few weeks later and I was devastated. He got what he wanted. In the late 00's, all my Asian female friends dated white men. My opinion is that they mostly like Asian women because many of us are subservient and a very loyal type of female. I have never been the subservient type. We aren't like many American women and tend to be more traditional in values. My Asian female friends wanted their babies to be half-white and that was the in thing to do. It was as if they wanted to start a new human race. When I went to Manhattan in 2014 to visit, all I saw was Asian and white couples. I thought I could be happy like them. Many of my friends were happy, but I think I just had bad luck with meeting the wrong men. Many men don't like independent strong thinking women."

Jaden follows Kim to her room and he stands by the door. She picks out some clean clothes. She leaves her room and walk towards her cousin's room. She has her clean clothes in her hand and Jaden continues to walk next to her. She opens the door and they walk in.

'Jaden, ask Kim if you can use that holographic disc on the table.'

"Kim can I use that holographic disc there? It is for something important," he says.

"Sure, that is a rewritable disc, it is probably blank. My cousin won't be back for a while," she says.

Jaden grabs the disc and holds it in his hand. She continues talking, "…anyway, my second boyfriend gave me chlamydia. He was Chinese and he cheated on me. The third boyfriend who was half-white and half-Japanese, used to hit me and verbally abuse me. My father found out and put him in the hospital. Then the abusive ex-boyfriend's family tried to sue my father in court, since they knew he was loaded. The point is I lost a lot of trust in men. They just lied so much and just wanted a trophy woman that they could treat like their property. I dated deceitful, narcissistic, and married men who said they were single. I had to put a high guard up around my feelings to protect myself from the emotional pain I suffered."

"I'm sorry he used to hit you, a man shouldn't be hitting a woman."

"It's okay. That made me stronger over the years," she says.

They finish getting dressed. Kimberly is wearing low cut blue jeans and a black and blue striped blouse. Jaden is

27

wearing some jean shorts and a short sleeve white button up shirt. He is trying on different sneakers.

"Made in China sneakers?" He asks. "I can't believe Michael Jordon is retired. I'm going to miss his sneakers."

"Yes, he was a legend. He retired at forty, eleven years ago. Now what was I saying? Oh yeah, over the last three years I stayed to myself. So many of my married and dating friends were catching STDs. It seemed like everyone was cheating on each other, even the women. I read online somewhere that ninety percent of men would cheat if they knew they could get away with it. Men are only truthful to their options. If a female wants a married man and the man knows he can get away with it, the option is there. If she was not around, there are no options. Men can get bored easily with one female. Men love adventure. Hookers and escorts do things house wives don't. Very sad but true, this is why the divorce rates are so high. Four years ago, two Japanese companies joined together. One specialized in realistic silicon dolls and the other was a robotic autonomous company. The robotic company had some advanced technology where they were able to mimic a real human brain. They were able to somewhat duplicate emotions and feelings. The new company created the first generation R.F.E.C. for men, but they had some problems and glitches. The second-generation entertainment companions were for gay men and women. The company promoted mainly to very busy hard working people and divorced women and men who were tired of going in circles in relationships. Their motto was, marriage lasts an average of two to six years, these robotic companions last a lifetime and will never cheat on you. They also claim their robots can do anything a spouse can do. That sold me into buying one."

They walk back into her room and they sit on the bed.

'Ask Kimberly what is the password for her secured wireless network.'

"Kimberly what is the WEP password for your father's 5.8 GHz wireless network?"

"Armageddon2032."

"What kind of password is that?" Jaden asks.

"That is the year Nostradamus followers forecast as the end of the world," she replies.

"Oh okay. Thanks for the password."

Kimberly continues her story, "When I graduated from college with my master's degree, my father wanted to buy me a new car. I told him to just give me $40,000 instead. I bought an R.M.E.C. second generation a year ago. These things have been selling out all around the world. Max has been my best friend ever since. Yes, I did have sex with him twice. But it didn't feel like the real thing, the small device in my lower back helped me to orgasm. Max was more of a woman pleaser and did whatever I asked him to do. It didn't feel real to me. I've always looked at him more of a friend than a lover…"

'We have to get out of here soon,' AI says.

"…around the same time last year, *Third Virtual Life* came out for men and women. Society has never been the same in regards to relationships between two people. Men stopped dating women and they could have all the sex they wanted in virtual life without a commitment. More women would date women and marriages declined. Newspapers in Virginia reported that groups of men would get drunk and have orgies with the R.F.E.C. robots. Gay men would have orgies with the R.M.E.C. robots. Pimps would pimp an R.F.E.C. for money and it was perfectly legal. Technology has really lowered society's values. So much has changed over the past ten years. Religious groups around the world got together and tried to ban the entertainment companions by saying you will go to hell for using the devil's sex tool to sin. They also tried to shut down *Third Virtual Life*, saying it was the devil's website straight to hell. Church groups published going to hell for dummies books."

"That's crazy. I can't believe society's values are slowly disappearing," Jaden says.

"More and more couples are having negotiated infidelity in their marriages to lower the risk of a partner cheating. The value of marriage is disappearing. Men want wives as nannies in that new bill they are trying to pass."

"What is negotiated infidelity?" Jaden asks in a confused voice.

"It's when married couples are allowed to have sex with other people. They do this to lower the risk of someone being unfaithful. These people figure it's better when both people know about it. The married female dates another man and has sex, while the husband waits in the other room. When it's his turn, he finds a female to date and have sex with in the other room. This is perfectly normal in these relationships. The wife sometimes even cooks dinner for her husband's date. This was on an episode of *Taboo*. These people blog about this and have fan groups for these types of relationships. What the hell?"

"You can't be serious. That is appalling and sick. But seeing it from their perspective, if it keeps the marriage stronger, maybe it's not a bad idea for them. If they both know about it, at least it is keeping them honest," Jaden says.

"Maybe you are right, cheating is the number one reason for divorce these days. Here is a quote from a famous female politician, 'Women need to change their conditioning, because there is no way men would change their nature.' "

"Nice!"

"I think females and women like myself are the ones getting the raw deal of this downward cycle. They created a new college course called Techsociety 101. Everyone has to take it before graduating with any degree, at any college," Kim says.

"What do they teach in the course?"

"To show how technology is changing society for the worst and how humans will eventually have no values at all. The beginning of robotic age was with the Sony AIBO dog in 1999, following the Actroid, ASIMO, Topio 4.0, R.M.E.C. and R.F.E.C. Robotic technology has forever changed life.

My dad bought me one of those Ers-7 AIBO dogs when I was younger. That was my companion as a young kid," she says.

"I remember, you brought that robotic dog on cruises and everywhere you went when you were an early teen," Jaden says.

"Max is a little overprotective and can get jealous, I've learned. This wasn't in the instruction booklet. His artificial intelligence autonomous programming is always evolving. He cooks, cleans, gives me massages, watches television and washes my clothes. Max has been the perfect boyfriend replacement. But the real emotions and chemistry aren't there as a real human. I can't connect with Max on an emotional and physical level. I have been able to talk to Max about science, politics, technology, current affairs, anything and he can talk about anything with me. He called me when I was in Albany a few times to see if I was okay. He is the best friend a female could have. It is too bad my father doesn't like him. When I go away on trips, Max stays at my father's house. They get along as friends, but deep down my father hates Max. He thinks the robot is getting in the way of me finding a husband and isn't real."

'We have to go, I just checked on the Internet that in Europe millions of people went unconscious. It is spreading as the sun sets. The end of the countdown is getting closer and Nanomoles are going positive and online. Thousands of people are disappearing on top of tall buildings. Radio telescope groups are picking up the location and giving the coordinates of the Darclonian's mother ship,' AI says.

Jaden explains to Kimberly as they walk downstairs. Three standard size UAVs are flying thousands of feet above the house. Jaden sees a watch on a table at the bottom of the stairs.

"Who's watch is this?" Jaden asks while picking it up.

"That is one of my father's old watches, you can have it. He buys a new watch every year," Kim says. Jaden puts it on his right wrist.

31

"Isn't the watch suppose to be on your left hand," she asks.

"I like to be different."

'I'm using all five nanoscanners to keep the agents and sniper asleep. It is about to wear off and they are waking up soon,' AI says.

"Would you like something to eat, *sweetie*?" Max asks.

"We are fine Max. You can call me Kim, Max," Kimberly says while looking at Max strangely.

"I don't understand, you let me call you sweetie all this year," Max says.

"Max, go to sleep," Kim demands.

"No, I'm not tired," Max says while walking away towards the living room to watch 3D television. They just look at him walking away.

"Sometimes he acts like a 9-year-old."

"We have to get to New York City as fast as we can to save my daughter," Jaden says.

"I don't want to leave without knowing where my father is," she says.

"Kim, if you stay here alone they will kill you. Bring a cell phone and we can keep trying your father on the way."

"Okay, I guess," she says while finding a spare cell phone.

"Did you know flights have been cancelled all over the United States since Saturday?"

"No."

"What kind of vehicles does your father have?" Jaden asks while they walk towards the garage.

"He has a few cars and trucks," she says while she opens the garage with her thumbprint.

They walk inside the huge garage area and the lights come on automatically. The smell of new car scent is in the air. Jaden's mouth is wide open and his eyes are fixated on one vehicle.

"We have a SUV, classic cars, a BMW, a Lotus and a Hummer."

"What is that!" Jaden asks loudly. He looks like a kid in a huge candy store.

"That… is a Bugattee convertible Mars special edition first generation. That wasn't on the menu of vehicles we can borrow. That car is my father's second child," she says.

Jaden walks over to it and touches the body. Touching the body tingles the Nanodrones in his fingertips. He feels an instant energy connection with the car.

"I've seen the commercial for this car, that night I was trying to escape from the hospital. 1204 horsepower, four independent wheel hybrid motors and a red carbon composite body. The battery is electro-nanomaterial and is inside the body and paint of the car…"

"No, no, no Jaden, you are wasting your time. We are not driving my daddy's 2.7 million dollar car. He would kill me if he found out. The insurance company charges each time it goes out of the garage and it has instant violations. Plus my father's fingerprint is the only print that can open the door and start it up. Let's take a BMW," she says.

Jaden doesn't take his eyes off the car. He looks at how low it is to the ground and the chrome vents on the hood of the car. The mind boggling LED lights on the front keeps Jaden's eyes on this amazing machine.

"Kim, we need something very fast to get to New York City. I will make sure there are no scratches or even a dent on your father's car. By the way, what does your father do?" He asks while continuing to stare at every inch of the car.

"He is a real-estate tycoon. Back in 2009 when the recession hit hard, my father bought some good properties when the prices were very low."

"Oh yeah, I remember now," Jaden says as he pictures himself behind the steering wheel.

'We have to go, the men are waking up,' AI says.

"Kim, this is the car we are going to need. We need something with run flat tires and a car that can run on electricity, gas or water. Trust me, there isn't much time."

"No, we can't. This is my father's baby...listen...." she pauses, "if you can get the doors open and start it up, then yes."

Jaden runs out the garage door like a child about to open his Christmas presents.

"I'll be right back," Jaden says with a huge smile on his face.

"There aren't any keys in the house! You are wasting time!" She yells.

She walks over to the BMW and opens the door. Jaden goes into her father's bedroom.

'Right there,' AI says.

'Perfect,' Jaden says.

Jaden runs back into the garage area with a huge smile on his face.

"Baby you are wasting time, let's just take this BMW here," she says while sitting in the driver's seat.

Jaden walks straight to the Bugattee sports car and puts his thumb on the door handle. The door doesn't open. He takes his hand off and tries it again. The door still doesn't open. The car begins to speak, "The car can only be opened by the owner's fingerprint. Another attempt and the alarm will go off."

"Jaden, that alarm will make a lot of noise if it goes off. Let's just take the BMW M1 here. It drives on hydrogen," she says.

Jaden looks at the BMW and then the Bugattee with frustration in his face. He goes for it and puts his thumb on the handle for a third time. There is a few seconds of silence and Jaden's heart begins to race. The seconds feel like forever. Kimberly looks at Jaden and covers her ears. The driver's door opens and flips upwards.

"What the hell?" Kim asks while standing up.

"Holy shit, a door that flips upwards, cool! What a future we live in!" Jaden yells with an excited look on his face. He stares at the door hanging over his head.

Jaden sits in the driver's seat of the Bugattee that makes him feel as if he is on the ground. His legs hang out of the side and on the floor. There are no rear seats. He starts the car up with another fingerprint button where the key ignition usually is. The engines roar at the same time, as if four lions are hiding in each wheel well.

"I am so low to the ground, I feel like I'm on the ground."

"Good afternoon, Mr. Chan. Today is, September 7th 2018 at 2:19 PM," the car says.

"Shit. Why did I have to tell my half alien boyfriend he could drive the car if he could get it open?" She asks herself aloud while closing the BMW's door, "That is like telling a car thief we can go for a joyride if he can steal this car." Kimberly walks towards Jaden.

'We have to go, soon,' AI says nervously.

Max walks to the garage entrance. Jaden turns the car off. He stands up and walks towards Kimberly.

"Will you be back shortly?" Max asks.

"Give this to Max," Jaden gives the holographic disc to Kimberly, "Tell him in twenty minutes to check the mailbox in front of the house and leave this holographic disc in the mailbox."

"Okay," Kim says while walking to Max and explaining.

Jaden sits back down in the car. He looks around like a child in a candy store. She walks back towards the passenger door, opens it and then climbs into the seat.

"What is on the disc?" She asks.

"A nanoscanner made a recording of the news reporter back at the courthouse. The Nanodrones then converted the recording over so that it could be saved onto holographic disc. We left an e-mail, telling her a copy of the story is in your father's mailbox at this address."

"Okay, how did you open the door and start the car?" She asks.

"I copied your father's fingerprint from a glass in his bedroom. A nanoscanner found the best thumbprint in his room and I put my thumb almost over it. The Nanodrones

35

matched the patterns and my thumb's fingerprint adjusted to his," Jaden says.

"That is almost unheard off and near impossible. I mean, wow, what can't you do? Are you going to take care of my father's Knight Rider?" She asks.

"Yes sweetie, I will take care of this like my own. This car is amazing. The instrument panel is around the edge of windshield. This is a car god, I've never witnessed such a beautiful car, " Jaden says while just looking around in amazement.

The rpm meter is on the left side of the windshield pointing up and down. The horsepower meter is on top and the speedometer is across the bottom in small bars. Two cameras are acting as side mirrors. There are small screens in the corners that show what is on the sides of the car. There is a huge screen in the middle console and a chrome stick shift lever between them that says QUADSMISSION. They put on their seat belts that come down like a roller coaster over their chests. He admires the camera side mirrors.

"The garage door opener is right there," Kim says while pointing at the button.

"We can leave in a minute. Myself and AI are calculating the distances around the body of this car using nanoscanners and Nanodrones. We are trying to properly align the distances and path the energy shield will take around the car while we are driving. But it is going to take some calculations and a few minutes. We both will have to control the movement as it moves around the car. Shit, the federal agents and the sniper are awake. It should be a few more minutes," Jaden, says while feeling the steering wheel and inhaling the new car smell.

"This car smells like an angel's breath," Jaden comments.

Nanoscanners are going around the car calculating every inch. The silent sensors in the doors of the house go off as the shield creating Nanodrones attempts to create an energy shield around the car. Jaden looks at the nine-inch LCD screen in the middle console.

"What color mood would I like my car to be today?" Jaden asks while reading the screen.

He presses on more info on the side and the car begins to talk.

"Your 2019 Bugattee is capable of changing to one of sixteen colors within seconds. Special polymers in the body contain paramagnetic iron oxide particles. Small electrical currents adjust the spacing of the small crystals within the iron oxide particles, giving the ability to reflect light and change color. Federal law only allows a vehicles color to be changed once a day and an e-mail or phone call must be made to your local police station, notifying them of the change."

"Wow, I didn't know that," Kim says.

"This car has the most advanced technology in it. I want to experience all of it. What did you mean earlier, when you said instant violation, Kim?"

'Jaden, by my calculations, the energy strength you have remaining isn't going to be enough. Depending on what the government comes after us with, we might not have the energy to withstand thousands of bullets or a few missiles, or even a big car crash.'

'We'll figure out something. Use that artificial creative mind you just created for yourself,' Jaden says.

"Instant violation is when the road or another driver can witness a traffic violation and you can get an instant virtual ticket with a court date. The instant violation program also includes receiving vehicle-to-vehicle text messages and your car speed recorded and sent to highway violation tickets. The program works; it cuts down on police traffic work and cities make a lot of money from the violations. Driving witnesses can come to court and make twenty-five percent of the traffic summonses, as long as they bring in their front car video recordings. Witnesses make fifty percent of the fines when they testify against a DWI driver. I had a DWI once, five witnesses came in to testify against me. They all split their half ," Kimberly says.

"Man, the future of driving doesn't look as fun anymore. But I'm sure I can make it fun today. You ready Kimberly?" Jaden asks.

"Yes."

"Quadsmission works just like regular stick shift right?"

"Yes, it does. The computer controls the amount of power in each engine, so that they work together."

'There are local police and agents outside,' AI says.

'I'm ready. I know this is going to require a lot of energy.'

"Max looks like he is about to cry sitting on the sofa watching television," Jaden says.

"I know. Don't tell me; he is too emotional for someone not human."

"What are these two red fingerprint buttons for, on the left side under the steering wheel," Jaden asks.

"I believe those are nitro buttons. In theory, the car is supposed to rocket beyond the maximum speed. My father wanted them specially installed. Why? I do not know. I think it was a waste of $150,000. He never used it and we won't need it, so don't worry about those buttons."

"I want to meet your father one day. I would love to talk to him all day about new exotic cars."

The garage door opens up and the Nanodrones are reflecting the light on both sides of the car. The car is in neutral and the engines are off. Jaden slowly presses on the brakes as the invisible car slowly moves down the inclined driveway.

"That is cool, you're making the entire car invisible," Kimberly says as she sees everything look refracted outside.

'Making this entire car invisible is draining your energy.'

The garage door closes back as they reach the end of the long driveway. Jaden has his finger near the ignition button. Suddenly there is a small glowing expanding circle of light showing in front of the car as a bullet stops in the energy shield around the car.

'Shit, don't hit the car, don't hit the car,' Jaden pleads to himself while he looks at it inching closer to the front windshield.

'Why aren't we using the forward shields?' Jaden asks.

'Being invisible works better with the reverse shields. I'm changing the direction now,' AI says.

"They know!" Jaden yells while pressing the ignition button and shifting into first gear.

The car roars like a monster and turns visible again. Jaden tries to turn the gearshift left and right but it doesn't work.

"I don't feel the clutch pedal and the gear shift isn't going into gear," Jaden says as five more bullets show up around the car.

"There is no clutch pedal and the gear shift is semi-automatic. Shift into D, then shift the gear to the right and use the plus and minus to change gears," she says panicking and pointing.

Two police cars approach. Jaden figures it out and the car peels off in first gear. He accelerates between the two police cars as they try to block him in. Jaden changes the gears quickly as he is doing 41mph on the small street. The car is roaring down the one lane, two-way traffic road. UAV aircraft are slowly following above.

"Shit, this feels awesome. I like this. I just don't like this futuristic gearbox. What are you doing Kim?" He asks while he watches her touch the front windshield on her side.

A medium-sized see through screen opens up on the windshield in front of her. She is touching the screen with her two fingers, changing menus and making things get bigger or smaller.

"I'm navigating through traffic conditions and checking my e-mail to see if my father e-mailed me. We need to get out of this area before rush hour."

"Cool."

Police cars and black trucks come up far behind Jaden. He reaches a stop sign at an intersection of a two-lane road and makes a right. He quickly accelerates as the aircraft above follow. There are only a few cars on the road. The car quickly goes invisible and Jaden slows down. He makes a U-turn and goes down the two-lane road. Jaden presses buttons on the center console screen. There is an image of the car with options for different body colors.

The car begins to speak, "Applying electrical current to body of car, adjusting crystals in the iron oxide particles in body. The outside of the car has been changed to metallic black. Please notify your local police, thank you."

"Yeah right."

The car goes visible again. The police cars and black trucks drive by in the opposite direction, along with the aircraft.

"Shake and bake!" Jaden yells with a smile on his face.

WASHINGTON, D.C. WHITE HOUSE 2:31 PM

"Yes, madam President it is a good idea you be with your family in Alaska. We are still trying to get to the bottom of this crisis. I can handle everything in Washington myself," Robinson says on the phone to President Stefanie Paylin.

"There aren't any aircraft flying in North America and parts of Europe. Are you sure what is happening in Europe won't happen in the United States? Also, are you sure it is safe to fly now?" She asks.

"I don't think you have anything to worry about President Paylin. Scramjet 1 is one of the best and fastest aircraft in the world. It can fly through any conditions. I think there is a connection between the terrorists in Virginia, what is happening in Europe and citizens mysteriously comatose sleeping. They blew up a federal prison, pushed a man off an airplane, assaulted officers, destroyed a courtroom and robbed a bank," Robinson says.

"I just want to make sure my family and grandkids are okay. I've lost contact with them. How accurate is the intelligence regarding the terrorist Jaden made threats against my family?" Paylin asks.

"CIA and FBI sources are saying there is great merit to the threat. They are still on the loose and are good at evading authorities," Robinson says.

"I trust your judgment and experience Vice President Robinson. You have my full consent to handle the situation and annihilate these threats against American lives," President Paylin says.

"Madam President, do I have your full authority to Motherdrone and the full usage of the military?"

"Yes, you do. I will let my cabinet and congress know as soon as possible. Keep me updated on everything that happens. I should be landing in Alaska in forty-five minutes."

They hang up the phone and Robinson sits back in his seat, lighting a cigar.

"Go protect your little sheep, mother sheep. Your assistant sheep is taking off his soft wool and revealing the wolf he really is. Baaah, Baaah, your baby sheep are calling for you. You weak excuse for a President. No experience in military, no experience in foreign affairs, and no experience with a national crisis. You couldn't run a presidency in your dreams," Robinson says while chuckling to himself.

ROUTE 360 HEADING WEST 2:37 PM

Kimberly and Jaden approach a red light and stop in the left lane. Jaden notices the rims continue to spin even though the car is stopped. In the lower left corner of the windshield, he sees the rims are producing electricity for the battery system of the car.

"We lost them, Kim. See sweetie, no damage."

"Thanks. There is no message from my father."

"I'm sure he is okay," Jaden says.

'If there is an attack, there will be four nanoscanners behind and over us at different angles. They will be able to

41

detect a fast moving projectile before it is fired. They will instantly communicate with the shield Nanodrones…'

A red and white Kawasaki motorcycle stops to the right side of Jaden's car. The man looks over and shakes his head up and down.

"Airbag system helmet?" Jaden asks.

"Yes, state law requires all people on motorcycles must wear these helmets that inflate into an airbag upon crashing," Kim says.

The man looks at Jaden and back at the light as he throttles his engine on the bike. Jaden replies with pressing up and down on the accelerator. He presses the button to open the hardtop roof. The roof quickly moves back and into the trunk area. He rolls down the passenger window.

"Jaden, don't race this man. Let's get to New York City in one piece, we are less than ten miles from the highway," she says.

'Jaden, you should listen to Kim. There are more police in the area.'

"Do you really think your new bike has a chance with this 2.7 million dollar car?" Jaden asks loudly over the engines, while looking at the man on the motorcycle.

'You have three miles of straight road ahead of you,' AI says.

'Thanks.'

The biker flips open the glass cover on the helmet.

"Let's go, buddy, let's see what you got. I have the fastest bike on this planet. That electric car has nothing on this modified Kawasaki ZX-16. Your daddy bought you that overpriced piece of shit electric experiment for use on another planet? You dickhead, there are no cars on another planet!" The man on the bike with a southern accent says. Jaden smiles at him, while thrusting his engine. The man continues and looks at the rims, "Dude, spinner rims were played out back in 2006!"

"These new turbine spinner rims are charging my battery system as we speak. We will see who leaves who behind when the light turns green cockrocket dude!" Jaden yells.

"Screw you!" The biker yells while sticking his middle finger at them.

"Can your bike do this!?" Jaden asks, while the outside body of the car turns white.

"Screw you fried chicken and green tea," he say while he press buttons and his bike's body turns pink and light brown.

"Pink is for the color of the inside of her pussy, and brown is the color of your little dick pretty rich boy. Your rich father should have bought your girl some more tits. Her little bitty titty committee needs to join a cohesive silicone titty committee!" The man on the motorcycle yells while laughing. Jaden stares straight at the man while the bike jumps forward and then back.

Kimberly shoots him a mean look for talking about her.

"Burn that dickhead," Kim says.

"Can you do this?!" Jaden yells at the biker while the entire Bugattee goes invisible.

The biker man looks in shock and he sees two middle fingers pointing at him in the air. Kimberly and Jaden put their fingers down and their hands disappear into thin air. The biker has a confused look on his face. The car reappears yellow before his eyes.

"Yellow is for the coward chicken shit look on your face!" Jaden yells.

"I love your mouthful little bitty titty committee twins," Jaden whispers to Kim, while staring at her and then the biker.

"Thanks baby."

The biker stares and waits for the light to turn green. Two cars approach from behind in each lane. The light turns green and they floor it, all five engines roar simultaneously. The car and bike take off like rockets. The Bugattee slightly peels off, but the traction control kicks in. The traction control on the bike does the same and keeps the front from lifting up. They take off neck and neck, while the bike is slightly ahead. The Bugattee's horsepower meter reaches 750 hp. They rocket to thirty miles per hour in a second. Kim's body presses against the back of the seat as she feels as if she is on a roller coaster ride. Jaden continues to stare at the biker and not look at the road, while quickly shifting the gears. There is a nanoscanner two inches in front of the side of his face showing him the road in front of him.

The wind is blowing around Kim and Jaden. They hit sixty miles an hour in 2.1 seconds as the bike rear wheel is at the front middle of the car. The biker leans his body closer to the bike. The Bugattee drops closer to the ground. They hit 90 mph and two windmill blades come out of the rear taillights on each side of the Bugattee. The two-foot long carbon fiber blades quickly begin to spin around the tail of the car. The Bugattee reaches 120 mph as the bike's rear wheel is at his hood. Roaring sounds of engines are the only things to be heard. Two images of windmill turbine kilowatt energy show up on the center console. HYPERCHARGED ENGAGED and REDUCING GAS USAGE shows up on the LCD screen. Electricity can be seen sparkling through the rims of the car.

Kim's heart is beating fast as they reach a quarter of a mile at 139 mph. The Bugattee and the bike are moving at the same speed, but the bike is still ahead. Jaden reaches 167 mph and slowly begins to catch up to the biker as the broken white lines in the middle of the street turn solid. Three state trooper cars driving in the opposite direction notice the drag racing. Jaden switches into sixth gear at 198 mph. Kim's hair is blowing in the wind as she slowly sticks a middle finger out the side of the window. The finger moves back and forth with the wind. The motorcycle's front wheel is at the rear of the Bugattee's trunk. They reach 214 mph and the bike is a car distance behind. Jaden suddenly hits the brakes and downshifts. The biker quickly passes by and he looks back at Jaden smiling. The hydraulic spoiler goes up to slow him down quicker.

"Dude, slow down!" Jaden yells, but knows the biker can't hear him. Jaden slams on his brakes harder and on the screen he sees the brake's kinetic energy charging the battery around the body of the car.

"Shit, what a rush baby!" She yells while leaning forward.

A state trooper car comes out of the bushes beside the highway and comes into the right lane. The biker turns around towards the road and sees the police car coming out in front of him. He brakes, while his body leans forward and smoke comes from the tires. The police car tries to back up, but it is too late. The biker hits the fender of the police car at 138 mph. The force and impact from the crash pushes the police car a few feet to the right. The biker's helmet airbag and body suit airbag quickly deploy as his body goes airborne. His body and clothes blow up into a big circular puffy airbag. His body bounces on the concrete as his bike flips over the police car in thousands of pieces. Crashing sounds echo in all directions. The biker's body slides on the ground as the debris falls in all directions. The nanotubing fender of the police car has no damage, just a scratch.

The police cars on the other side cross the grassy median and quickly accelerate. Jaden slows down to 20 mph and drives into the grassy median. He slowly goes over the motorcycle debris as the windmill blades on the rear continue to spin. The top of the car comes out of the trunk area and back over the top of the car.

"Is he okay?" Kim asks.

A nanoscanner checks his condition. The officer runs towards the biker laid out on the highway.

"He is breathing without any broken bones. That body airbag really saved him. That was wild, the poor guy," he says while driving back on the highway.

Instant violation shows up on the LCD screen.

"There is one witness and three police officers that will show up for court for drag racing at: 2:38 PM, on Highway 360. Your court date is set for October 7th 2018. You are

45

hereby found guilty and have to prove yourself innocent in a court of law. You have 6 points on your license Mr. Chan," the automated computer says.

"Jaden, that went on my father's driving record. Shit, my dad is going to kill me."

'That wasn't wise to race that motorcycle. The local police saw the drag racing and reported our car. Now the government knows where we are. They also know that the car changes colors,' AI says.

'I know, it is a male testosterone thing, you won't understand. But it was such a rush. This car is unbelievable. It produces huge amounts of electricity from mini windmills for the four engines at high speed. The electricity was going straight into the engines. That is unbelievable, I have to see the fastest this car can go.'

"Sorry about that," he says.

"The police are gaining behind us Jaden," Kim says while looking through the side mirror screen.

"I know baby, I know."

"You do realize you can leave the gear shifter in drive and the car will change the gears by itself and it is just as fast as manual?"

"Manual and automatic transmission? Cool," Jaden says while putting the gear in D.

"Your welcome baby, drive safe," she says while holding Jaden's right hand.

'There are more jet fighters, police helicopters, news helicopters and many police cars coming this way. There are also more vehicles on the road ahead. Your body is not going to have enough energy soon, you are at twenty percent now. We need to figure out another source of energy to use,' AI says.

'One Adam, multi highway infrared license readers confirm license plate VA CHANMAN has terrorist suspects in vehicle. They are driving west on Highway 360 in a yellow Bugattee sports car. The vehicle has changing colors capabilities…' Jaden hears through the nanoscanner in a police car 500 feet behind him.

'All police vehicles are made with nanotubes and liquid metal materials. That is why you didn't see a dent in the police car when the bike hit it. That material would require the forward shields to use more energy to destroy it and using higher rpm,' AI says.

'I saw on my eyes a few minutes ago, you were showing me an animated simulation of using reverse and forward shields?' Jaden asks while driving back and forth between lanes around cars at 60 mph in a 40 mph zone.

'Yes, using them both around the car in two different directions with some magnetic Nanodrones in the middle, I came up with a new weapon we could use. When the two opposite direction moving energy shields touch, they would explode outwards in all directions creating an electromagnetic pulse wave. This will knock out anything electrical within a one mile circumference,' AI says.

"Will you accept incoming vehicle text messages from other drivers?" The car's computer asks.

'What about the car we are in? Wouldn't it lose power also?' Jaden asks.

Kimberly presses the accept all button on the LCD screen for incoming vehicle text messages.

'This car will be in full shield mode. Meaning the wheels and underbody will be covered by the forward shields, protecting the car from the pulse wave. The energy required would use ten percent of your energy,' AI says.

Messages show up on the top of the windshield and scrolls across in see through white letters: SLOW DOWN YOU ASSHOLE, THIS IS A SCHOOL ZONE. I'M REPORTING YOUR LICENSE PLATE. SHOW SOME RESPECT FOR OTHER DRIVERS. PRICK! PRICK! PRICK!

"Wow, these drivers are getting pissed off," Kim says.

The police cars quickly catch up behind Jaden. Vehicles slow down and let the police cars pass through.

"Pull over and turn your engine off," a police officer says through a loudspeaker in a cruiser. Other vehicles on the road get out of the way. Three other police cars are behind Jaden as he accelerates. Police send a car text message to Jaden also.

"A red light coming up, baby," Kim says nervously.

Five cars are sitting at the red light, while many vehicles are crossing back and forth through the intersection. Two nanoscanners are in the intersection looking in both directions timing the vehicles. AI is doing high-speed calculations. Jaden slows down and drives onto the shoulder on the left while police cars follow. A news helicopter is hovering above, following the Bugattee. Kim turns the radio on and listens to some 00's music on satellite radio.

A news reporter is talking into a microphone, "We are live on a high speed police chase. Known terrorist Jaden Marino and his female accomplice are in a stolen white Bugattee driving west on the 360. They are approaching a busy intersection and are slowing down on the shoulder. It looks as if they are apparently giving up. Oh wait, they just quickly accelerated through the red light and narrowly missed a delivery truck and three passenger cars. The Bugattee just caused two accidents in the intersection as cars slammed on their brakes. The police are stuck at the intersection trying to go around the cars."

'Excellent timing on that one AI.'

Jaden quickly goes around some cars and turn onto a ramp to drive onto Interstate 295 north. Light traffic is on the three-lane highway as Jaden quickly accelerates and merges into traffic. The news helicopter continues to follow above.

'I have an idea. Can we somehow use the Gravhawk for assistance?' Jaden asks.

'Using the Gravhawk for air support to take out aircraft is not...' AI says while Jaden interrupts him.

'I know, I know, it can only be used for emergency purposes. I'm talking about using it from where it is now, some way. There should be a way to transport more energy to where I am now.'

'The first problem is I would have to be in the Gravhawk to operate it. The second problem is that your mind will not be able to do all the high-speed calculations alone to control the moving shields. Even if you could, your mind could overload and go into shock, causing you to have a seizure, destroying brain cells and/or putting you into a coma. The third problem is we would need instant communication to where the Gravhawk is near the North Pole.'

'Shit, that isn't good. Well at least figure out the instant communication issue and how you could get the energy to me if you were in the Gravhawk,' he says.

WASHINGTON, D.C. PENTAGON 2:45 PM

Robinson is deep underground in a room looking out a glass wall with a special helmet on his head and face. Robinson just finished doing a full hand, eye, voice and DNA scan. There is very advanced computer equipment in the room. He is looking at huge 200-inch 3D images outside the glass. Military personnel are walking around outside the room, across an elevated walkway. There is a huge light rod going from the ceiling to the floor towards the right of the small room. Beams of light are moving up and down the rod. Robinson is communicating with the supercomputer through the helmet by thought.

The female voice of the supercomputer begins to talk, "Next generation of defense activated. Supercomputer Motherdrone is now online. Third generation prototype quantum synthetic diamond processor is clocking at 500 petaflops a second. High-speed communication airship blimp is online. Communications test to satellite and then to airship blimp is 0.10 seconds. Total time to UAVs from blimp, 0.50

49

seconds. Geostationary blimp is at 71,500 feet and moving over situation area."

Robinson goes through the menus by just thinking about it.

"Please select threat. Terrorist threat selected. Please select the level of the terrorist threat. Maximum Osama Bin Laden threat selected. Please select civilian casualty percentage. You selected seventy-five percent, Motherdrone will be cautious of civilian life twenty-five percent of the time. Property damage and infrastructure damage are at twenty percent protected. Target is located on satellite driving north on Interstate 295. Tank drones, helidrones and UAV wolf pack are online. Autonomous mode is offline and being fully controlled by Motherdrone. Threat will be annihilated in less than ten minutes. Would there be anything else sir?"

"Yes, use the prototype rail gun tank drones. This is the perfect time to test our new powerful top-secret weapon in the real world. Let's see how this terrorist stands up against 9000 mph magnetically charged projectiles."

"Yes sir. Have a good day President K. Robinson."

"Time to sit back and watch the fireworks in 3D," Robinson says jokingly.

VIRGINIA INTERSTATE 295 NORTH 2:47 PM

Kimberly and Jaden pass huge billboards on the right of the highway. The wind is blowing through the open windows. Jaden reads the words on the huge billboard, "Join a class action lawsuit against cell phone companies? What did cell phone companies do to people?"

"Cell phone companies have been putting cell phone tower antennas on top of buildings and near people for years. The last five years, people have been coming forward after getting tumors, cancers, miscarriages, multiple sclerosis, immune illnesses and children with birth defects. Cell phone companies has since united together and put airship blimp cell

50

phone tower antennas at 65,000 feet all around the country to avoid future lawsuits," Kimberly says.

"Damn, that sucks," he says.

"Cell phone companies are also being sued for selling higher radiation 4, 5 and 6G cell phones to consumers. Brain cancer cases increased forty percent over the past twenty years."

Jaden thinks about all the people suffering with brain cancer. His eyes wander to another billboard.

"What is this billboard about? Harry Potter fans would enjoy *Terry's Nightmares* trilogy now in paperback in stores?" Jaden asks.

"That is a new book series by author V. Carter, I read some of his stuff on ebooks. It's pretty good, he wrote the Trialien trilogy a few years ago and he helped direct the movies of the books."

"Oh, okay. Interesting."

'Three police cars are quickly approaching. I came up with a resolution for the communication problem from the Gravhawk. I can communicate to you through the crust and mantle of the planet, by using solar neutrino particles,' AI says as the Bugattee increases speed.

'What are neutrino particles?'

'They are particles that mostly come from the sun and can pass through any material. There are trillions of them passing through us and through the planet as we speak. They are smaller than Nanodrones, and are around the same size as nanoscanners.'

'Cool, did you have any ideas on getting me some more energy?' Jaden asks AI while police cars pull up behind him doing 85 mph.

'Not yet. But I calculated the energy shield to be open at the front near the intake air vents of the car, so the vehicle can have the proper airflow.'

'That's good AI.'

The Bugattee drives ahead of a pack of cars and is in the middle lane.

"Be careful baby, police cars," Kim says.

"Pull over now! Pull over! This is your last warning!" The police yell over a loudspeaker.

Jaden increases his speed to 102 mph as the windmill blades begin spinning from the taillights. The energy shield recalculates around the car to avoid destroying the windmill turbine blades that just came out on the rear of the car.

"They are attempting to do a PIT maneuver on us baby," Kim says.

"I can't believe they still do this. Let them try their fishtail maneuver," he says with confidence.

The first police car quickly pulls up on the right and the other two are a few cars lengths behind. A nanoscanner overhears the news helicopter reporter above giving his commentary live on the air.

"...the police car on the right is attempting a PIT maneuver to get the high speed sports car to stop. He is going for it, the front of the police car is about to hit the rear of the expensive white stolen sports car. I hope the owner has good insurance for that car... What the hell? There are awkward flashes of light at the front of the police car as it hits the sports car. This is unbelievable ladies and gentlemen, half of the hood is completely obliterated. The police car is spinning out of control, grinding against the ground and crashes into the concrete guardrail. The other police cars avoid the out of control car. The wheels are ripped in half. Oh my god I can't believe what I just saw. The sports car is in fact slowing down so the cop cars can catch up..."

'That felt good at 300,000 rpm shield speed.'

'Your energy is getting lower and lower,' AI says.

More police cars are approaching quickly from behind as Jaden passes an entrance to the highway. A state trooper car stops about a mile ahead of the Bugattee and gets out of his car. A second police car approaches again on the passenger side of the Bugattee. Jaden continues to drive in the middle lane at 80 mph. The car on the right tries to smash into Jaden from the passenger side. Abnormal bright light flashes around the left side of the police car. Kim screams from looking at all the bright light to her right. The officer pulls to the right away from the sports car. The officer hops and quickly climbs into his passenger seat trying to avoid the light particles near him. The officer is still holding on to the wheel as the car slows down. Jaden's energy shield destroys a foot into the nanotube body doors. The third police car falls back.

"Did you see how fast that officer jumped into the passenger seat of his car? That was like watching an old episode cartoon of Scooby Doo. When Scooby jumps into Shaggy's arms when he sees a ghost," Jaden says.

"I couldn't see it, I had my eyes closed," Kim says.

'There is something in the middle of the road quickly approaching us. It looks like some kind of...'

'It is some kind of a net device. Full shields!' Jaden quickly yells as they are about to run over it.

The energy shield fully surrounds the outside of the car and quickly wraps around the underbody and wheels of the car. The Bugattee wheels begin to spin faster since they aren't on the solid ground. The X-net crossing the highway jumps off the ground as the car goes over it. There is a flash of light under the car as the X-net is destroyed by the energy shield. There is an explosion of threads and materials going into different directions. The shield quickly goes off. A state trooper looks at the Bugattee quickly going by and can't believe the car beat the system.

"What was that baby?" Kim asks.

"Some kind of car net stopping device. It jumped from the ground to wrap around the wheels. I thought they were tire spikes, but I was wrong," Jaden says.

There is a roadblock two miles ahead as the Bugattee goes invisible. They take an off ramp and get off the highway. They go visible again as the helicopter continues over the highway.

"Did you see that what I just saw? The car went over the police department's Tru X-net system and then the car disappeared into thin air," the news reporter says.

"I've seen those nets on police shows, and they stop vehicles one hundred percent of the time," Kim says.

"Well now it is ninety-nine percent of the time," Jaden snaps.

"Off route, recalculating," the car navigation says. "Drive five miles and take ramp onto Interstate 95."

They reach a red light and the car goes visible again in the color blue. On the other side of the ramp, police are blocking off the entrance to get on the highway. Jaden runs the red light and makes a left turn onto a two-lane street.

'AI, I have an idea. You remember how the nanoscanners connected together to communicate when I was landing the 737 airplane?'

'Yes.'

'How about using the nanoscanners from the Gravhawk to connect together, to somehow transmit constant energy from the magnetosphere to me. The atomic solar recharge receives its energy a similar way right?' Jaden asks.

There is a pause as AI does calculations. A nanoscanner sees the traffic coming from different directions before he reaches the intersection

Jaden reaches a four way stop sign and goes through it at full speed.

"You have exceeded your maximum car color changes for the day. You will receive a fifty dollar fine for each violation in the mail," the car computer says.

Police cars come from all directions and down the ramp the Bugattee just came from. Jaden sees heavily armed drone aircraft coming from a distance. He quickly accelerates on the six lane two-way street quickly moving around cars.

'Yes, that just might work. It is kind of risky, but we can do that. Kim will be exposed to high radioactive energy, so I came up with an idea to fix that. Your nanoscanners and Nanodrones will have to create a filtering energy matrix above the car to send it down directly into your body. That is something we can do, but we still have the last problem. You can't control the high-speed calculations needed for the shield system with your mind alone. I can't be at two places at the same time,' AI says.

'AI I can handle the calculations myself. I have confidence I can multi-task, control the directions and movement of the shield generating Nanodrones. I'm not going to overload my brain. I've done the impossible until now, I have the confidence that I can handle it.'

'Are you sure? There could be irreversible damage to your brain,' AI says.

'Yes. We don't have too much of a choice anyway, I need your assistance friend,' Jaden says.

'Okay, sir. I'm updating the Nanodrones now and preparing for flight. If you don't survive, I'm suppose to come back to fully destroy your body and then return to Xenos right away.'

'Yeah, I know. '

Vehicle text messages bombard the windshield from other cars: WTF! YOU ASSHOLE, YOU JUST RAN A STOP SIGN WITHOUT STOPPING. I VIDEO RECORDED YOU AND I'M GOING TO REPORT YOU. I HAVE CHILDREN IN THE CAR, SLOW DOWN. I'M REPORTING YOU FOR RUNNING 2 STOP SIGNS, UNLESS YOU GIVE ME AND MY TWIN SISTER A RIDE IN YOUR HOT SPORTS CAR. 704-555-3091.

Jaden peaks over and his eyebrows raise. The last vehicle text shows an image of two hot young females.

"Damn these easy materialistic southern bitches," Kim says in an upset tone.

She presses some buttons on the LCD screen and begins to talk.

"Listen you two easy, gold digging bitches, you can ride on my two fists. Get a life, he is taken," Kim says while pressing send.

Her words convert over into a text message and are sent out. Jaden and Kim laugh to themselves.

"Wow baby, you are like a pit bull, defending property. That is crazy, women picking up men in the future. Times have changed, baby. I didn't know you could send messages back to people also, that is cool," Jaden says.

"Yeah, you just need the first letter or number of the license plate. Someone can also point a device at a car to send a message," she says.

Jaden is still driving around cars and just went through a yellow light.

'Are you ready to leave, AI? I'm at twelve percent total energy.'

'Yes, I'm lining up the nanoscanners to slingshot me north. I have microscopic proton thrusters to guide me, when I slow down from 0.001% the speed of light. It should take me a few minutes to reach the Gravhawk and another few minutes to setup the Gravhawk's nanoscanners. When I leave your body, you will feel a tingling sensation in your brain. When using full shields around the car, remember not to have the forward shields destroying the ground you are going over or you can crash into the ground. Just guide the shield generating Nanodrones around the specified dimensions of the car and they will do the rest. The faster you guide them, the faster the rpm. Concentrated shield energy is needed in one area of the shield to destroy material at a high rate of speed. Just in case you crash into something, you won't damage the car. A faster rpm requires more energy and more instant destruction. They can be expanded out as far as you want and they can go around something else. It is all about mind control and multi-tasking. Good luck Jaden,' AI says.

'Thanks I'm going to need it,' Jaden says while he continues to speed around cars changing lanes, doing 75 mph in a 35 mph zone, while still receiving vehicle texts. AI shrinks in size and leaves Jaden's brain. He feels a tingling sensation as AI leaves. Jaden feels a cold loneliness as he realizes he has to do everything by himself. He feels as if he is Captain James T. Kirk from *Star Trek* and quadrillions of Nanodrones are his crew or the apprentice just promoted to Jedi. Jaden knows he has to do the impossible.

He tries to psych himself up with his eyes in a trance, 'I am the lawnmower man, I am the lawnmower man.' Nanodrones start a diagnostic test on Jaden's eye screen, 210 BILLION ENHANCED NEURON CELLS AND 12 TRILLION SUPPORTING GLIA BRAIN CELLS ONLINE. ARTIFICIAL SYNAPSES AND AXONS NANODRONES ON STANDBY FOR NANOTIME. CHEMICAL NERVES, NANODRONES AND BRAIN IMPULSE SPEED AVERAGING 5200 FEET PER SECOND.

Jaden explains to Kim that AI went back to the Gravhawk to help him with his energy. Kim tries to relax while holding on to Jaden's right hand. She knows Jaden concentrates better with loud music, so she changes the radio satellite station to rock and roll from the nineties. Seven police cars quickly approach from behind. The loud sirens sound in all directions as passenger vehicles move out of the way. Some police cars are driving on the other side of the street and some in the service lane. A police helicopter hovers right above the Bugattee with a dual mini gun. Officers in three of the cars begin shooting towards the tires. The bullets disappear into the forward shield as Jaden continues to concentrate on the rpm speed. A drone aircraft is approaching from above as well. Jaden quickly approaches a busy intersection at a red light. His nanoscanners are looking at the traffic in both directions, but Jaden can't calculate what speed he should go through the intersection at to avoid an accident.

"The hell with it," he says while accelerating on the broken white line in the middle of the street, squeezing between four cars stopped at the light behind each other. A missile is shot from the UAV Predator drone with a lock on the Bugattee.

The Bugattee passes the solid crosswalk line as it enters a bi-directional one-lane traffic intersection. Jaden's brain goes into nanotime 100x, as he reaches 375,000 rpm. Three-fourths of the shield goes around the car. Jaden gets creative and sends anti-gravity Nanodrones around the outside of the shields to soften the impact. Kim takes her hand from Jaden's and covers her eyes with both hands. A flashing bright camera light comes from behind the Bugattee as the red light camera goes off, taking a picture of his license plate. A blue passenger car approaches from the left and a green minivan from the right. The driver of the blue car tries to slam on the brakes, but smashes into the left driver side of the Bugattee. Light particles light up around the Bugattee. A glowing translucent energy travels around the Bugattee from the impact area. The blue car leans forward from the momentum and the energy shield instantly destroys some of the front end of the car.

Kim feels the powerful jolt on the car and a shock wave goes through her body, pushing her towards Jaden. She begins to scream while holding onto the dashboard and grasping the handle on the door with her right hand. The air briefly comes out of her lungs. The force of the hard impact absorbs into the two layers of the shield and moves the entire Bugattee. The first layer of the shield protects the body of the car. The impact force pushes the Bugattee's rear towards the right into a tailspin. The blue car's rear is lifting up from the ground, while broken glass, metal, and debris is flying into the air in slow motion. The missile slowly inches closer towards the Bugattee. The zero gravity around the Bugattee causes the blue car to flip upwards into the air from the rear. The Bugattee is spinning out of control and crashes into the minivan. The passenger side of the Bugattee smashes into the left side of the minivan heading in the opposite direction of the blue car. The second red light camera flashes capturing the chaos. The minivan's left side is slowly destroyed as the force of the impact pushes it into the sidewalk. Half of the minivan driver's body rips away. Debris is flying upwards into the air. The Bugattee is spinning in circles inside the energy shield. Kim and Jaden feel the powerful forces around them. The seat belts tighten their grip around them. The wheels are spinning out of control without any traction creating smoke all around the outside of the car.

The Bugattee's windshield is displaying information, ENHANCED STABILITY CONTROL ENGAGED, TRACTION SYSTEM ENGAGED.

The blue car with a missing front end does a somersault just missing the fast moving missile. Jaden concentrates on expanding the shield out further around the car as his nanotime goes off. The blue car lands upside down and skids on the ground. The minivan smashes into a bus stop, destroying it. The Bugattee is still spinning with forward momentum onto the other side of the highway. Pro-gravity Nanodrones are under the car trying to slow it down. Jaden braces himself and tells Kimberly, "Brace yourself."

The missile hits the front of the spinning Bugattee head on and there is a loud explosion echoing in all directions. Kim bangs her head on the passenger side window from the powerful force. Fire explodes around the translucent lightning-colored particles. The force causes the shield to implode towards the inner shield. The Bugattee is moving faster out of control. The concrete rips away behind the spinning Bugattee. A huge fireball spreads around the entire car. The Nanodrones in the shield counteract the fire and force. The streetlight overhead explodes towards a wooded area to the left. A shock wave of energy goes in all directions. Other cars in the intersection burst into flames from the explosion. The Bugattee changes directions towards the right of the road and heads towards a storefront, still spinning out of control. A nearby tree catches fire while a light pole is ripped in half by the energy shield. Simultaneous car accidents follow as other cars slam on their brakes and smash into other cars on fire in the intersection. People walking near the intersection are running away screaming. The police chasing behind Jaden stop before the intersection and witness the destruction in front of them.

The Bugattee crashes into the front entrance of a store. There is a loud crash and Kim bangs her head on the side of the passenger window again, this time from the sudden stop. Kim's ears begin to ring as she opens her eyes to look around.

People run out of the side entrance of the store. The shield goes down around the car. There are dildos and blow up dolls falling onto the hood of the car. There are two guys face down in a *Third Virtual Life* machine. There is a black material over their bodies as if they are in a body suit. The two men continue in their virtual world and don't realize a car just crashed within a few feet of them. Kim and Jaden take deep breaths. Jaden looks to his left and notices the big hole through the store.

Kim hears a familiar voice, but it sounds far away, "Kim, are you okay? You okay baby?"

Kim looks around in a slight daze as she rubs the side of her head. She looks Jaden straight in the eyes and smiles.

"I'm okay, just banged my head up a little. You sound far away. I'm surprised we survived the car crash and missile. I think the loud explosion from that missile really hurt my ears. I thought the shields around the car absorb loud sounds also," she says while her voice echoes to herself.

"Sorry sweetie, the shield's energy can't deflect all the sounds."

"Okay."

"Hang in there baby, I don't want anything to happen to you. What kind of store is this?" He asks.

"Wow, I can't believe we are still alive. Everything happened to fast," Kim says while opening her eyes.

"Baby, what kind of shit is this? These two guys are strapped into *Third Virtual Life* and they are having a threesome with a virtual R.F.E.C. unit. How sick is that?" Jaden asks.

WASHINGTON, D.C. PENTAGON 2:55 PM

General Peters walks into the small room where Robinson is standing with a huge grin on his face watching the huge screen. Robinson is watching his predator lock on to the Bugattee entering the intersection.

"Is this live sir?" Peters asks.

"Yes," Robinson replies.

The missile has a camera on it as it cruises right over a police helicopter. It goes under a blue car flipping forward and hits the fast spinning out of control Bugattee. The video on the missile becomes static as the Predator drone continues recording from a distance.

"Sir, the Motherdrone just fired a Hellfire missile in a local U.S. city," Peters says.

"Yes, I know," Robinson says.

"What is the civilian casualty percentage set for Motherdrone?" Peters asks while he sees cars on fire and cars running into each other.

"Seventy-five percent," he says while watching smoke coming out of the store.

"Sir, what are you doing? There are going to be many innocent citizens killed at that high percentage. You can't do this," Peters says.

"Don't tell me what I can't do. Jaden is a terrorist and needs to be removed from the face of this planet. He has been a nuisance to me for the past eighteen years. He is the cause of the problems we are having around the world and he is the reason for these conspiracies."

"Sir, that is not true. We are getting intelligence that he is here to help us. We have testimony from a Marshal Lopez that Jaden Marino is a hero and saved Flight 104. Scientist Dr. Kimberly Chan and her team have found a foreign organism in human brains that is causing people to lose consciousness. This is confirming the information we received weeks ago from the unknown source in space," Peters demands while looking directly at Robinson. Robinson's face turns red with anger as he watches the Bugattee drive out of the storefront without damage.

Robinson turns towards Peters, "Listen Peters, I don't have time to hear this bullshit. This man is the problem and he is heading to Washington to attack the Capitol. He manipulated our LRSB to create this hoax somehow. The aliens that took him are in his body and they are all part of this conspiracy."

"Sir, where are you getting this information from?"

"Listen Peters, you have been by my side for the past twenty-five years. I'm pulling a lot of strings for you to get your hearing early for secretary of defense. General Peters, are you aware of the New World Order program?"

"Yes sir, I am. New Mars World Order program is still over one hundred years away. It involves terraforming Mars to be a second Earth and creating a new law system there. What does that have to do with what we are talking about?" Peters asks.

"Plenty, there is a New Earth World Order at the beginning stages now. You didn't have clearance for this intel before. Microchips in people, DNA of every citizen on record, everyone being monitored, swine flu microorganism shots, technology overtaking society and microtransmitters in money. This is all the beginning stages of the New Earth World Order. The human population needs to be controlled better. Outsides or the unknown can be a threat to this process," Robinson says.

"I can't agree with all those tools being used on our own American citizens. Religion and keeping a certain amount of fear in Americans has been the best strategy of choice over the years. Scaring the public to an extent to have more money for defense is plausible. However, painting Jaden Marino as a terrorist and putting this type of fear in the American public is not a logical strategy. Threat level red is not needed for this. People are confused enough with all the headaches and sudden sleeping. This isn't the time and place to scare the public even more. We know the helmets block out this invisible signal to human brains. I don't understand why you are going after someone innocent and putting American civilians in harm's way."

"I don't have to explain myself, Peters. I don't need some alien terrorist getting in *MY* country's way."

"Your country?"

"Yes, my country."

There is a pause as Robinson and Peters look dead into each other's eyes.

"Sir, why did you have the Buckeye Federal Prison destroyed?"

"Peters, destroying the prison was also a part of my New World Order plans the government has been preparing. This is the beginning of it. This is what you call instant justice and saving the taxpayers billions of dollars. I packed hundreds of prisoners from Guantanamo Bay; the terrorist from the Jet Ski attack on lower Manhattan in 2015, serial killers, death row prisoners, drug dealers and terrorists on long trials all in that one building. No one saw the missile attack and we put the blame on terrorist Jaden Marino. Martyr terrorists want to die anyway, I just gave them what they wanted. Seventy-five percent of the prison was on death row also. We will rebuild that one building for a couple of million dollars and save billions in the long run. It is a win-win situation and justice is served. I call it T.N.W.M.M.M. or The New World Modern Money Mechanics," Robinson says.

"Sir, that doesn't even make any sense. This isn't justice, this is killing humans who deserved a fair trial..." Peters is interrupted by Robinson.

Robinson frowns, turns red and gets angry. He slams his hand on a table and kicks a chair and looks Peters in the eyes.

"You don't tell me shit about justice! I served this country all my goddamn life! This is how I'm going to run this country! I watched while the greatest prison, Guantanamo Bay, was shut down in 2010. I watched real justice done on criminals at that prison. We were able to do whatever we wanted to get answers out of prisoners or terrorists. Those prisoners were happy to commit suicide by the time we finished with them. This court system and justice system in America is outdated. The Constitution is an outdated joke. We need a new world constitution and it needs to start somewhere! We waste countless money on long trials and criminals having too many rights! Every time I take a shit, I hear of some criminal beating the system. I'm making that start and getting rid of anyone who gets in my way. This man Jaden Marino is a loser alien with magical powers. If we kill him, I bet all these problems around the world will stop," Robinson yells.

"What if you are wrong sir?"

"I'm one hundred percent sure, if not I'll still be relieved that the little bastard that cost me my career promotion eighteen years ago is still blown to pieces."

"So, this is a personal vendetta between you and this teenager?"

There is no answer and Robinson takes a deep breath.

"Sir, the countdown is real. This half-alien kid can help our military forces greatly. If our soldiers can do a fraction of what this kid can do, we can be the superpower of the world again. We can invade any country we want and use economic hit men on China and other countries we owe money to. Our spaceships could reach light speed within the next ten years. We can make private space travel a thing of the past, if we can learn this advanced technology. Jaden is the key to learning this. This teenager traveled 4.2 million light-years in seventeen years and he is the same age as when he left. Killing this kid will be a very big mistake," Peters says.

"I do not trust this kid, if we don't destroy him now, he will take over our planet. His alien friends sent him here to take over human civilization and killing him will stop this silent attack on humans. I need you to trust me on this one. Peters, I need to know if you are going to be by my side. I'm guaranteeing you will make secretary of defense next week, I need to know if you believe in what I believe," Robinson says.

"Sir, you have changed over the years. You've gotten worse and worse with your judgment. Now you are killing innocent and guilty people. You have taken the law into your own hands. Jaden is someone here to help us. This isn't what I stand for and not what America stands for. You ordered the shooting down of Flight 104 because you thought Jaden took over the flight. You denied a possible military SWATbot air boarding. You are killing innocent civilians on your war campaign with Jaden Marino. You turned Area 51 into a new age universal Guantanamo Bay. I can't follow this dark path you have chosen. You lost your morals and your humanity. I understand the court system doesn't work, but it is up to the people and congress to change that. It is not up to you or us to decide who should live or who should die. I followed you all my life and I was always by your side. But, now I stand down. I don't want the secretary of defense position if it will be under you and your new vision," Peters says disappointingly.

"You are relieved of your duty, General. That is the problem with this country, weak humans with morals and emotions trying to run it. America needs strong leaders to make real decisions like myself. I'm one of the few vice presidents who weren't a politician. This country doesn't need money hungry politician puppets being manipulated by big corporations. You keep our conversation between me and you, unless you want your name smeared and to be court-martialed," Robinson says.

"Yes sir," Peters says while saluting Vice President Robinson.

Peters turns around and walks towards the door.

"That is the problem with America today, it is run by nothing but pussies that aren't about any type of change!" Robinson yells while looking at the screen.

"At least these pussies have some value of human life," Peters says while stopping with his back turned.

"I always looked at you with higher regards than my own son. Even though my son is a senator, he has always shared my values and beliefs. Goodbye General Peters," Robinson says.

Peters walks out the door.

Robinson turns and looks at his wolf pack of UAV drones flying together towards Jaden's location.

Jaden is nervously awaiting communication from AI. Kimberly is using her cell phone in an attempt to reach her father. Jaden is down to three percent total weapon energy as the Nanodrones slowly recharge themselves. There is silence in the car and the engines sound in the background. The windmill blades on the tailspin like two fans at a distance. Jaden is a few miles from Interstate 95 and he comes up with an idea. There is a Mustang car tailgating the Bugattee at 75 mph.

More car text messages show up on the windshield, YOU ASSHOLE, I'M AN OFF DUTY POLICE OFFICER. I SAW YOU RUN TWO RED SIGNAL LIGHTS AND DRIVE RECKLESSLY THE LAST FEW MILES. STOP YOUR CAR NOW.

The off duty police officer's Mustang is tailgating the Bugattee. Jaden reads the windshield and looks in the rearview mirror. He slams on the brakes and Kimberly leans forward, dropping her phone. She braces herself and the Mustang runs into the Bugattee's rear energy shield. The force of the impact makes the Mustang lift from the rear and flip over the completely stopped Bugattee. The front of the Mustang disintegrates and lands upside down in front of Jaden. The car grinds on the highway upside down.

"What was that for Jaden?" She asks while reaching down to grab her cell phone.

"He said stop my car now."

Jaden quickly accelerates to the still grinding upside down Mustang and rolls down his window. The officer is bleeding from the top of the head and mouth. What is left of the car stops in a grassy median and is smoking from the front. Jaden stops directly on the side of the car in the left lane.

"Let's go Jaden, don't stop here," Kimberly pleads.

"Are you okay, *Officer stop your car now?*" Jaden asks while looking at the officer struggling to climb out of the passenger side door. He crouches on the other side of his Mustang and quickly draws his gun and fires at Jaden. The officer groans and breathes heavily while he shoots.

Three shots ring out at Jaden from a 9mm Glock. Kimberly braces and covers her face.

The bullets stop eight inches from Jaden's left leg. Jaden puts the Bugattee in park, opens his car door and it flips up. He takes off his seat belt and turns his body towards the officer. The bullets fall towards the ground and Jaden's left foot is outside the car touching the ground. Kimberly holds Jaden's shoulder to keep him from leaving the car. The officer looks shocked. A few cars pass by and look towards the upside down car. Jaden's eyes are turning darker.

"Those bullets were shot kind of low. If this was target practice officer, you wouldn't score in any percentile!" Jaden snaps.

"Jaden stop this, let's go," Kim pleads.

"Hold on a second, I don't want to leave the scene of an accident, without checking on this officer of the law," he says to her.

"Officer! I don't get a *Freeze! Step out of the car with your hands up?* What is this, the days of shoot first ask questions later huh?"

The officer is in shock and doesn't respond. His right hand with his pistol is aimed at Jaden and shaking.

"Sorry to see you hurt, but if you had your seat belt on you wouldn't have banged your head on the windshield and steering wheel like a test dummy!" Jaden yells.

The officer fires another two shots at Jaden. The sound of the bullets is muffled behind Jaden's energy shield. The bullets stop six inches to the right of Jaden's stomach. Police sirens can be heard coming from a distance. The bullets hit the concrete highway and roll with the rest.

"Come on officer, you can't aim for my heart or head? All those years at the firing range? I'll give you another try," Jaden says in a playful voice and a smile on his face. His eyes become completely black.

Jaden takes his fingers and points one finger at his heart and the other in the center of his head. The officer aims his gun and unloads his gun at Jaden. Kimberly looks out of her window and braces herself. There are six bullets around Jaden's heart and six around his head. Jaden now hears the clicking of the gun. Kimberly looks out of her window and sees a circle of smoke near the shoulder lane. She quickly takes off her seat belt and looks over at Jaden's right hand going up.

"You see that officer, good job. Good shot, you would have killed me. But let's see how good my aim is on the first try." Jaden says in a serious tone.

Kim reaches down towards the brake pedal and shifts the gear shifter into drive with her right hand. The Bugattee jerks forward and Jaden grabs the closing door above him with his left hand. He brings his left leg back into the car and the door closes. He looks at the road in front of him and steers the car, while accelerating. He puts his seat belt back on.

"Why did you do that?" Jaden asks.

"You were going to kill that officer!"

"No I wasn't, I was going to hit his car and make it spin around some," Jaden says as his eyes turn back to blue.

"What is getting in you? We don't have time to be messing with a police officer."

"You like how I was able to activate the shields by the time the officer clicked his trigger?"

There is thirty seconds of silence as Kim looks through the windshield ignoring Jaden.

"That was kinda cool," she responds a few seconds later.

Jaden quickly accelerates again as his overall weapon energy goes down to two percent.

"I don't know what came over me back there. Thanks for getting us out of there, baby," Jaden says.

"It's okay, don't worry about it."

A minute goes by and Kimberly asks, "What idea did you come up with a few minutes ago?"

"I'm still waiting for contact with AI and my energy is getting very low for the outside shields. Can I put my hand over your eyes again? I need you to tell me what you see in the nanoscanners. Multi-tasking with the shield and driving is tough enough," he says.

"Sure, baby, I'm happy to help out in any way I can. I feel like I'm in *Third Virtual Life* here with you. They have a part in *Third Life* where you run from the police in the game and if you are caught, you feel hits with sticks from police all around your body. It's cool seeing through the nanoscanners, when I see through things they look like an animated cartoon. But I feel so protected next to you," she says raising the volume on the music. Jaden covers her eyes with his right hand.

They turn onto the ramp for the I-95 expressway north. Jaden notices parts of the highway are made out of some futuristic aqua green material. A Nanoscanner passes through the material to determine what it is. The wheels driving over them make a weird ruffling sound.

"Kim, what are these patches in the highway? I'm scanning hydrophilic glass compounds."

"They are called solar roadways and states are replacing damaged highways with these solar panels embedded into the highway. In the future, they would produce electricity for entire cities."

"Cool."

"There is a FBI helicopter coming up from the right and two military Hummers with huge guns a few cars behind us. There is also a pack of about, one, two, three, four, ten, fourteen aircraft approaching a few miles from the north. They look like UAV drones and F-35's," Kim says while looking through multiple nanoscanners.

"Okay, thanks baby," Jaden says while Kim licks his thumb with her tongue, "Damn, baby you turning me on with that tongue.

"This feels as if you are blindfolding me baby and we about to do something freaky," Kim says in a sexy voice.

"Hold that thought for later," he says while looking towards her smiling.

They merge into traffic and drive in the middle lane of the three lanes. Huge tractor-trailers are in the middle lane of the highway, following behind each other. The Bugattee quickly moves from lane to lane and in between the trucks, cutting off vehicles and quickly accelerating to 89 mph. The Bugattee moves around the cars and vehicles as if they are standing still. Cars are swerving and people are blowing their horns as they are cut off.

WTF repeats on the windshield message screen.

"What does WTF mean, baby?" Jaden asks.

"It is something bad, I'll tell you later," she says while giggling.

"This is like playing the game *Q*bert* and *OutRun*," Jaden says with a smile on his face.

"*Q*bert? OutRun?*"

"Oh boy, it is before your time Miss Pokemon generation."

The Bugattee cuts off a red SUV by a few feet. The SUV swerves into the right lane hitting another car. They lose control and other cars run into each other. Sounds of smashing metal and wheels locking up echoes behind them. There is a six car pile-up. One of the military Humvees is struck by a passenger car and stops. The second one continues driving at high speed on the right shoulder as more cars approach. There are two huge guns on the roof being controlled by a computer and pointing at the Bugattee about 900 feet away. One of the huge guns has thermobaric air explosive bat bullets, and the other is a nanorocket launcher. The Bugattee is changing lane to lane and quickly going around vehicles at high speed. Loud sounds of skidding wheels are all around them. The bat bullets lock on to different areas of the Bugattee. Slow moving bat bullets are shot at the Bugattee. The bullets take different directions around the moving vehicles on the road. Some bat bullets go under tractor-trailers and some quickly change direction

70

around passenger vehicles. The dozens of bat bullets have small wings on them and thrust energy coming from their rear. The bullets are passing under moving vehicles and over cars towards the fast moving Bugattee moving at 92 mph. The bullets quickly speed up spraying the outside of the Bugattee's first layer shield. They create explosions all around the car. Thumping sounds can be felt throughout the car. The energy shield around the car glows with translucent light particles around it. Some of the bullets ricochet into different directions and explode on other vehicles. The Humvee slows down and falls back, while the Bugattee speeds up to 115 mph. Vehicle text messages continue to flood the Bugattee's windshield.

"The FBI helicopter is about to fire something towards us, I can't tell what it is," Kim says. Jaden continues to pass around cars and trucks. The FBI helicopter comes up over the Bugattee. Jaden activates his shields as an agent on the helicopter fires a microwave beam towards his car. His shields absorb the powerful waves and then reflect them in the same direction. The helicopter begins to lose power and control. The engines make a malfunctioning sound. Jaden's energy goes down to one percent.

"Shit, we are dead baby. My weapon energy is almost depleted."

"Baby do something quick, a wolf pack of UAVs are getting closer."

A soldier on the back of a military hummer begins to fire a mini gun at the Bugattee.

Jaden has another idea as he sees cars flying past him in the far left lane. As the traffic approaches in front of him, he goes over towards the entrance lane of the HSCCVL. The FBI helicopter crashes into a nearby schoolyard.

"Baby, what are you doing? We can't drive in the computer controlled vehicle lane, the system isn't installed in this car. My father can get tons of tickets and this expensive car can be disabled by an electric shock disabler," Kim says.

"Don't worry baby, that might be the shock we need. I think your father's license is the least of our worries," he says, "The local police are being told to back down."

Jaden drives into the lane. He sees letters scrolling across a sign on the overpass above and a car text shows on his windshield, PLEASE EXIT THE HSCCV LANE, YOU ARE AN UNAUTHORIZED VEHICLE.

The other cars behind the Bugattee in the HSCCV lane automatically slow down and go into the small idling lane to the right. The super HSCCV computer is driving the cars for miles ahead onto the right shoulder and vehicles are put in neutral. The opposing HSCCV heading south is also shut down.

"You have five seconds to comply or risk thousands of dollars in damage done to your car's electrical system," the car speaks.

"More like hundreds of thousands of dollars in damage to the electrical system," Jaden says while chuckling.

Kimberly has confidence in Jaden. A powerful electrical charge comes from an overpass sign and from a rail on the left divider. The electrical charge enters the outside shield. Electricity lights up the outside shield area. The Nanodrones convert the energy over and Jaden's weapon energy goes up to four percent. A missile is shot from the first UAV. Jaden accelerates to 98 mph and then to 121 mph as he passes cars idling on the right shoulder. Drivers are being advised to sit in their car until further notice. The missile hits the concrete divider twelve feet behind the Bugattee creating a huge explosion. The force propels the Bugattee's tail upwards and then back down. The shield system absorbs the explosion. Jaden's weapon energy goes down to 0.1%. The UAV also begins to fire a machine gun at the Bugattee.

"You are driving seventy miles over the speed limit in a HSCCV lane, you have just received three instant moving violations. Your court date is set to January 14, 2019. Please slow down now," the car says.

"Hey! That's my birthday, will I be twenty or thirty-eight?" He asks while trying not to panic.

"Good question," she says.

"Shit, we are doomed. That last bullet penetrated and hit the right rear tire. I'm down to a weak first layer forward shield. What happened to AI?" Jaden asks.

Jaden increases his speed to 140 mph as he passes cars less than two feet on the right side of him parked in the service lane. The UAV circles to come back around. There is a small spark of light outside the passenger and driver windows. The side mirror camera LCD screens turn black.

"Shit, I controlled the shields around the car too close to the body and took out the side mirror cameras," Jaden says.

"You didn't really need them right?" She asks.

"Not really, but they did look cool. I'm trying not to damage your daddy's car. I have to make sure I don't destroy the windmill blades on the back. I'm trying to make sure enough air is passing through them also."

'……..' Jaden hears static, 'AI?'

An older man is sitting in his expensive Mercedes in the service lane, to the right of the HSCCV lane.

"This is bullshit, all this money I'm paying a month to use this HSCCVL system and I've been sitting in the same place for the past five minutes. How long does it take to disable one car driving in this lane. It is probably some immigrant that can't read English driving in this lane," the man says to his wife sitting next to him. He grabs the door handle.

"Hubby darling, the system says stay in your car and don't open the door. Where are you going? Stay in the car," the man's wife says.

"I want to see what is going on and if I can see anything from here," he says while pulling the door handle and flinging open his door.

The Bugattee quickly approaches the Mercedes at over 160 mph. The Bugattee quickly rips off the man's door. Concentrated atoms ripping Nanodrones are in the impact area of the shield. There is a loud roaring sound swishing by. Broken glass falls on the couple. The couple is shaken by the fast moving car and the wife screams. The man holds his chest as if he is about to have a heart attack. The door is launched into the air and off the highway.

A nanoscanner goes into the ground in front of the Bugattee to transmit Jaden's communications back. Jaden slows down to 105 mph.

"Why are we slowing down?" Kim asks.

'Hey, Jaden can you hear me okay?' AI asks.

'Yeah I hear you! Where you been buddy? I'm down to 0.1% energy left. I'm feeling weak and tired. What is going on?' Jaden asks.

"Don't worry Kim, I have a plan."

'I was trying to establish the correct neutrino speed and frequency to…' AI says.

'Don't worry about it, explain that to me later. Have you established the magnetosphere link with the nanoscanners?' He asks.

'Yes, that is complete and they are online. They are above the Earth and around the magnetosphere trying to lock in on your signal. There is so much satellite debris and garbage floating in space. It is like a junkyard on different subspace levels around Earth.'

"Baby! The wolf pack of UAV drones just fired several missiles towards us!" Kim yells while flinching.

'Hurry up and lock in now! They just fired nine missiles at us!'

Jaden takes some deep breaths. His eyes focus on the road completely. He looks as if he is in a trance. He concentrates on what he has to do.

"Let's see what these last three gears and turbo button have," Jaden says while he takes his right hand off Kim's eyes.

"You are driving forty-two miles over the speed limit, your license has been suspended until the year 2018 and a warrant has been issued for your arrest. Your insurance has been notified," the car computer says.

AI is preparing the Gravhawk's nanoscanners to shoot a beam of unfiltered energy from the magnetosphere down to Jaden in the Bugattee. AI is having calculation problems with the distance, movement of Earth and the alignment from the magnetosphere. Three of Jaden's nanoscanners are circling around each other above the fast moving Bugattee as the car reaches 102 mph. The nine missiles get within 500 feet of Jaden. Jaden goes around a slight curve on the highway and he sees a few miles of straight road.

"Shit, I can't wait on AI. Time for plan B. Hold on baby, it is Knight Rider turbo boost time. Let's see what this 2.7 million dollar car can do," Jaden says as the missiles get within seventy-five feet of him.

"Hold on tight!" He yells.

He shifts gears, floors the pedal and presses the red nitro button. The car drops an inch from the ground. The Bugattee propels forward at breakneck speed. Their heads and bodies press hard against the seat and headrest. Jaden's eyes are wide open and his adrenaline kicks into high gear. The digital speed readout on the windshield quickly moves as if they are getting gas at the pump.

"Holy shit!" Kim screams with her eyes closed as her body takes a few G forces against her seat.

"Yeah baby! This is what I'm talking about!" He yells in a trembling voice.

She clutches Jaden's right leg and her right armrest with her hands. The force pushes her heart into her back. Jaden has a huge smile on his face as his body vibrates. The horsepower meter reaches 1204 and the car's rpm reaches the redline. Jaden quickly shifts into the last gear and electricity can be seen in the slowly spinning rims. The Bugattee accelerates to 240 mph and then 272 mph in seconds. Jaden keeps the steering wheel very straight. Kim's heart is beating very fast as everything looks like a blur around her. She digs into Jaden's leg with her nails. A violent wind shakes the idling cars to the right, as the Bugattee zooms by them at lightning speed. Their cars pull inwards towards the HSCCV lane from the powerful wake. A light grey haze is coming from the four wheel wells of the Bugattee. The missiles hit the ground and concrete behind the car, just missing it. Concrete and debris flies in different directions.

The ground rumbles like an earthquake over and over again. Huge explosions of fire spread in several locations. A highway sign that says 95 WASHINGTON D.C NORTH falls onto the highway in flames. Huge craters form all around the highway. Light poles topple onto the other side of traffic. Two idling cars are hit and explode. There are several huge explosions as a cloud of fire reaches hundreds of feet in the sky. The Bugattee quickly passes the other cars sitting in the service lane. Jaden keeps the steering wheel very straight as the highway overpass goes by in the blink of an eye. The vehicles driving on the main part of the highway look as if they are sitting still. The engines are roaring as if jet engines are in 10.1 Dolby sound. An air vacuum under the vehicle is sucking the Bugattee to the ground and keeping it from taking off into the air. The windmill blades behind the car are spinning like helicopter rotors. The windmill blades, spinning rims and micro turbines around the Bugattee is contributing eighty percent of the car's power to continue at this high speed. The news helicopter flying above is trying to catch up. Five drone aircraft fly closer to ground level and under an overpass. Two more are above the opposite highway lane dodging cars. Seven are spread out in formation about seventy-five feet above the highway. The car reaches 295 mph and messages show up on the windshield screen.

"Maximum speed attained. Tires overheating, injecting liquid nitrogen into tires," a female computer voice says. A male computer voice speaks, "You are driving 230 mph over the speed limit. Your license has been revoked until the year

2026. There is a warrant out for your arrest. Please turn yourself into the local police station. Your vehicle ID has been sent to the authorities. Your insurance carrier has cancelled your policy."

"I can't open my eyes! I feel like I'm on a roller coaster!" She yells.

"Shit, there is a…" Jaden says.

A dancing R.F.E.C. unit is standing in the HSCCV lane next to a passenger car a few miles in front of the Bugattee. A man in his early thirties and his teen daughter are watching from the car window as it dances to some music playing from the car. The Bugattee slams into the R.F.E.C. at 279 mph ripping the robot into several thousand pieces in all directions. Vehicles on the highway are receiving car texts and phone texts to exit the highway.

"What was that? What did we hit?" Kimberly asks with her eyes closed.

"That is for ruining society's values and trying to replace women, you wanna be mommy substitute. It was an R.F.E.C. with a skirt on. Shit, they are locking on to us again," Jaden says.

"Hey! Those R.F.E.C./R.M.E.C. units are helping lonely people and preventing lesbianism," she says.

"You should know, with your ex-boyfriend Maximilian," he snaps.

"Hey," she yells while hitting his leg.

Jaden reduces speed and talks to AI.

'AI, where are you buddy? I can't drive any faster and I can't outrun directly fired missiles.'

Kim is still talking, but Jaden doesn't pay attention to her.

'Any second now, the gravitational pull outside the magnetosphere and the planet rotating was interfering with…' AI says going in and out with static.

'Just charge me! Save the explanations for later!'

The UAV drones lock on to the faster moving target and simultaneously fire several missiles at the same time in the direct path of the fast moving Bugattee.

Jaden's eye screen reads, NANODRONES REPORTING CATASTROPHIC IMPACT AT 0.5 ENERGY STRENGTH.

Most of the vehicles on the main part of the highway are in the right lane and trying to exit. Vehicles idling in the service lane to the right of the HSCCV lane are being told to manually drive off the highway. Jaden concentrates on his speed and shield rotating. He knows he can't outrun the missiles again since the UAVs are directly behind him. A nanoscanner is detecting a 7000 lb thermobaric bomb in a stealth bomber quickly approaching a few miles in front of them. High-speed missiles quickly approach Jaden. He can hear the loud thrust of several missiles. They pass right through a nanoscanner and Jaden can briefly see the electronics inside a missile.

"It's time to pray Kimberly! Hold on!" He yells.

A nanoscanner shows the materials in the thermobaric bomb as fluoridated aluminum and other explosive components. AI has a lock and the powerful energy is shot down towards Jaden at a quarter the speed of light. Jaden is watching his weapon energy screen still at 0.9% strength. His mind instantly goes into 100x nanotime and the car slows down to 140 mph. Everything is happening in slow motion for Jaden. His weapon energy accelerates from 1.1% to one hundred percent. Jaden feels the energy going into his body and back out into the clear shield around the car, reinforcing the layers. His signal strength from space is at seventy percent as he goes under an overpass. A huge invisible shield expands around the Bugattee in the shape of a circular mushroom, it stretches out to twenty feet and retracts. All two layers of the forward shield are online. The first missile explodes twelve feet behind the Bugattee and is absorbed into the shield. The force of the blast causes the car to swerve. There is a loud thumping sound and the car shakes. Kimberly screams from the impact.

All the UAVs pull up into different directions. Two missiles hit the ground around the Bugattee. The rest hit the energy shield directly. There are several loud explosions.

Fire is completely around the shields and Jaden's human eyes can't see the road. The powerful force causes the car to tailspin and scrape the concrete divider. His energy strength quickly drops as the shield-producing Nanodrones try to counter the explosive energy. The force of the missiles quickly passes through the shield and makes the Bugattee spin out of control. The full shield around the car doesn't give the car any traction to the ground. It crashes through the concrete highway divider on the left and goes into southbound traffic. Debris, fire and metal flies in different directions. Everything is happening in slow motion for Jaden, but very fast for Kim as the car reaches 82 mph in out of control 360° spins. She feels the car spinning and pulling her body in different directions. The vision from the front windshield is a blur to Kim. Her hands leave Jaden's leg and arm rest and slowly move towards her face. She is screaming in a low growl. A yellow cab is directly in front of the Bugattee.

There are several cars quickly approaching the Bugattee. The outside shield is still on fire as the vehicle spins into the middle lane. The full shields around the wheels disappear and smoke comes from the tires as they spin on the pavement. Jaden turns the steering wheel the opposite direction of his high-speed counterclockwise tailspin. Jaden doesn't panic and knows he can't disintegrate an entire vehicle coming towards him. He tries to quickly figure out his options. Messages are showing up on the windshield, but Jaden doesn't have time to read them. He does advanced calculus calculations in his mind while he pumps the brakes. Jaden comes up with a solution. The yellow cab doesn't have time to react. Jaden changes the angle and direction of the shield around the Bugattee. He calculates the rear of the Bugattee will hit the front of the cab in 0.3 milliseconds. The shield takes the form of a ramp and scrapes the concrete highway. Pieces of the white line scrape into the shield. Jaden concentrates on a smooth ramp shield with anti-gravity Nanodrones over the top of the Bugattee. The rear slowly turns towards the front of the taxi. Pro-gravity Nanodrones go to the sides of the Bugattee to counteract the out of control spinning. The taxi driver slams on the brakes and turns to the right, but it is too late. The look of fear is present in the face of the driver as he runs into the Bugattee head-on. The yellow cab lifts into the air on a 20° incline. The bottom of the wheels are disintegrated as the car goes airborne at 68 mph. Kim's hands finally reach to cover her face. The Bugattee reaches the right lane of the southbound traffic still spinning out of control. A female driver in a blue car lets go of the steering wheel and covers her face screaming as she runs into the side of the Bugattee. The car is lifted into the air by the shield ramp. Pieces of tire and metal go into the air as well. The fire around the Bugattee is gone.

The Bugattee breaks through the concrete divider on the right hand side of the southbound highway. They are on top of an overpass. Jaden sees it is about twenty feet to the ground and quickly gains control of the vehicle. The back wheels are off the highway and are spinning in the air. Concrete falls down to the street below. The Bugattee is skidding and the shield is destroying more and more of the highway divider. The front wheels pull the car back onto the highway and Jaden continues driving north into southbound traffic. Nanotime goes off and the yellow cab lands on the highway without any wheels. Sparks and debris are under the cab as it grinds on the pavement. The blue car is airborne and doing a backwards flip forty feet in the air. Kim opens her eyes and looks around. She is dizzy and disorientated from the fast spinning movement. The Bugattee is at 20 mph.

"Holy shit, that was amazing! What a rush!" Jaden yells.

Jaden drives on the shoulder. Other vehicles slam on their brakes. The blue car lands head first on the highway. Broken glass lands everywhere. The blue car's airbags deploy. Fireballs continue to explode upwards not far behind Jaden.

"That lady is going to need an ambulance quick."

"What happened?" Kim asks.

Jaden's concentration is on the parachute bomb just deployed from the stealth bomber.

"I'll tell you later. We have to get out of here! Quick!"

He turns back onto the southbound lanes of traffic driving north. There is a minivan coming straight towards them.

"Watch out!" Kim yells.

The minivan turns to its right hard and is about to flip over on its own. Jaden drives directly towards the tipping van. Jaden hits the minivan and it spins sideways in the air and over the Bugattee. Jaden turns hard right and drives through the concrete divider. He is now in the northbound HSCCLV. He quickly accelerates in the HSCCLV. The airborne van quickly tumbles down the highway.

Jaden floors the gas pedal to try to get in front of the thermobaric bomb about to land on the highway. The Bugattee reaches 108 mph as vehicles on the highway are moving to get off the highway exit. He reaches 151 mph and he calculates he will beat the bomb to the ground. The Bugattee quickly passes under the huge bomb and passes an oil tanker in the right lane. Suddenly the bomb explodes forty-five feet above the highway. There is a loud deep explosion that echoes in all directions. The energy waves of the huge explosion jerks the Bugattee forward while the full shield goes on. Kim covers her eyes again. The air sucks towards the powerful oxidizer explosion like a vacuum tornado. The green highway sign over the highway is pulled towards the explosion and rips off the support beams. A fireball spreads in all directions engulfing everything. The explosion spreads to other cars on the side of the road, quickly engulfing them. The air in the area quickly turns into flames. Fire is all around the shield as the tires lose traction to the ground. The force is pulling the car backwards.

"Hold on baby, that second blast is coming."

The oil tanker behind the Bugattee explodes and that blast makes the car spin out of control. Whitish orange fire incinerates and kills people in their vehicles. Highway signs are ripped off and pulled towards the initial blast. Concrete is exploding into the air. The ground shakes as if there is an earthquake. The nanoscanners circling above the Bugattee move up higher. There are several loud bass explosions. Bright yellow and orange fire is everywhere. The powerful shock wave is felt over the Bugattee as the outside shield absorbs the high kinetic energy and explosive pressure coming downwards. The Bugattee begins to slow down as the forces pull it back towards ground zero of the huge explosion. Everything is being sucked into the area above the bomb blast. The shield Nanodrones are counteracting the vacuum and high explosive forces. The air pressure increases in all directions around the Bugattee. Jaden's weapon energy goes down to sixty percent and then forty percent as he increases his rpm to 341,000. His mind starts to hurt as he overloads it. The strong forces destroy the second layer of Jaden's outer shield. Air is being sucked out of everything in a mile circumference. The momentum of the Bugattee has slowed down to 81 mph as it continues to spin in circles. Debris is flying over the Bugattee. There is a huge inferno on the ground as the fire rises upwards. His nanoscanners signal strength goes down to fifty-one percent.

The fast spinning is causing Kim to get dizzy. She screams from the fast spinning.

"Stability control two engaged," the car says.

Different sides of the vehicle's brakes randomly go on and off.

"Quad traction sync engaged."

The wheels spin out of control while the tires create smoke from the friction of the tires on the inside shield. The oxygen inside of the car gets very low. The full shield is trying to keep the pressure in the vehicle stable.

"Baby, hold your breath!" Jaden yells. Kim takes a deep breath and closes her eyes and mouth.

Three different beeping sounds are going off in the car. The nanoscanners above the explosion detect a temperature of 3200°F inside the huge explosion. The Bugattee's momentum slows down to15 mph.

"Zero traction, hyper stability control engaged. Oxygen is low, switching to full battery power. Unfamiliar terrain. AC offline and outside temperatures exceeding 160°F," the car's female voice says. "Please select which planet you are on."

The center console shows local planets in the solar system. They ignore the flashing screen.

"It is getting very hot baby and I'm getting very dizzy. I can't take all this spinning around," she says while she begins to cough.

The Bugattee's spinning slows down.

"Hold on baby, don't talk. I'm trying to counter the forces and figure a way to get some traction on the ground," Jaden says while unbuckling his seat belt.

"I can't breathe and my ears are beginning to pop. I'm burning up in here," she says while struggling to breathe. She looks out the window and sees fire burning all around her. She panics in her mind, but tries to keep it together.

Jaden reaches over and unbuckles Kim's seat belt. Sweat is dripping down her face. The Bugattee straightens out on the fiery road still in Jaden's full energy shield. The Bugattee is still pulling backwards as Jaden's weapon energy goes down to fifteen percent. The Bugattee's wheels are still slightly spinning without traction.

Jaden looks Kim directly in the eyes as she continues to cough, gasping for air.

"I'm going to breathe in your mouth pure oxygen and then you are going to hold your breath for at least one minute. Okay?" Jaden asks while leaning closer to Kim. She nods her head in confusion. Jaden has his left hand tightly on the steering wheel. Pure oxygen enters Jaden's pores and then into his bloodstream. The oxygen then goes through his capillaries in his lungs and his chest expands. He presses his lips against hers. He breathes into her lungs and she holds her breath.

"Baby, climb over and sit on my lap. I'm going to have some Nanodrones regulate some cooler temperatures around the outside of my body," he says while she takes off her jeans and quickly moves her sweaty body to his lap. Her legs are on the side of his waist as she faces him, blocking the fiery view in front of him. He closes his eyes and relies on his remaining nanoscanners. She quickly takes off her blouse and unbuttons his shirt. She rubs her chest against Jaden's cool chest. Jaden has his left hand on the steering wheel and eyes shut. She embraces him with both arms around his neck and he puts his right arm around her back. Jaden feels her heart beating fast next to his.

'Get out of there Jaden! The charging energy isn't properly passing through the explosion,' AI says.

Fire is burning hot all around the Bugattee's low shield as sweat is running down her chest and back. The car is trying to make it up a slight hill. Jaden uses the anti-gravity Nanodrones around the rear of the Bugattee to balance the vacuum forces pulling the car backwards. Cooler temperatures are circulating around Jaden and Kim's bodies. Jaden is also creating stable pressure around Kim's body. He is concentrating heavily on his shield speed moving around the car. A determined look is across his face. Drips of sweat run down his face as his brain is at eighty percent usage. Rock and roll music is playing in the background. Jaden concentrates on creating an opening in the shield around the front wheels. The pressure increases in the car as more air sucks from the front of the wheels. The two front wheels touch the 1100°F concrete. The wheels quickly spin while the rear tires are still inside the energy shield. The vehicle senses the increased temperatures and injects liquid nitrogen into the front wheels. The rear wheels stop spinning and all the power goes to the front wheels as the traction system engages. The temperature increases in the car. The tires quickly spin on the concrete creating forward momentum. Fifty-five miles per hour is registering on the windshield.

"Maximum battery speed attained," the computer says.

The car is moving at 12 mph. Kim feels air being pulled from her mouth and nose. She begins to gasp for air again. He feels her heart beating faster and faster against his chest. The UAVs are hovering back and forth over the huge mile long fire on the ground using sensors to detect the Bugattee in the inferno. Another missile is shot through the fire and hits behind the Bugattee, destroying the ground and giving the car forward momentum. The car lifts up into the air from behind. Jaden holds onto Kim tightly as their bodies lean towards the windshield. The rear of the Bugattee is three feet from the ground and the front scrapes against the shield energy. Pro-gravity Nanodrones keep the car from fully flipping forward. They are riding on two wheels. Jaden's brain is in full multi-task mode as Kim has her hands tightly over her eyes. She coughs and gasps to breathe the hot air around her. Jaden quickly breathes his last breath of air into her. The car accelerates forward and out of the fire zone. He makes it to the top of the slight hill. Smoke trails the quickly accelerating Bugattee.

The fire around the shield extinguishes as the sunlight returns and Jaden's weapon energy quickly goes back to one hundred percent. The full shield goes off and the AC comes back on in the car. Jaden and Kim take deep breaths. The hill begins to decline and clouds of fire can be seen behind them. The cold air hits Kim's sweaty back and feels so refreshing. There are some military vehicles on the highway and Jaden drives around them. They fire bat bullets from the gun turret on two Humvees.

"Baby are we still alive?" She asks while opening her eyes and looking at Jaden driving with one hand with his eyes closed.

"I'm fine baby, just have a slight headache, besides that I'm fine. Can you breathe okay? How do you feel?" Jaden asks.

"I'm okay now. I felt as if I was being burnt alive. I never felt such intense heat. I felt like I was in an oven. Do you need me to move baby, so you can drive?" Kim asks.

"No, you can stay right here. I want you close to me. I'm using a nanoscanner to drive, this reminds me of the PC game *Test Drive* I used to play in high school with the different camera angles and views. My human eyes are good for seeing full menu screens for my body and weapon systems," Jaden says.

"All this near death, fire outside the car, explosions and high speed driving is turning me on baby. You protecting me like a superhero and saving my life has gotten my kitty cat very, very, wet sweetie," Kim says in a sensual voice while kissing Jaden's left ear and neck.

"Wow, baby, your panties are soaking wet. You're catching me off guard here..." Jaden stops while Kim kisses his lips and tongue.

The Bugattee is swirling over the highway trying to avoid the bat bullets. The bullets hit the car and small explosions occur, making the car jerk up and down. Kim's head and body moves up and down.

Jaden disrupts the gravity around them so Kim doesn't feel the sharp leaning forces of the car. His energy continues to go up and down on impact, but it stays near one hundred percent. Two UAV drones are flying behind the Bugattee at ground level. One is flying at ground level in the opposite traffic direction. Five others are flying eighty feet above the highway. The UAV drones begin to fire synchronized machine gun fire. Flashes of light precede bullets hitting the car from different directions. The powerful shield absorbs and deflects thousands of bullets. Passenger vehicles are approaching ahead on the highway as the Bugattee reaches 144 mph. The shield expands outwards like a mushroom as he continues to change lanes. Kim continues to kiss and grind her wet panties against his pelvic bone.

"...You giving me a lap dance at high speed?" Jaden whispers while slightly moaning.

"You like it?"

"Yes. This reminds me of my first strip club when I turned eighteen last year. I mean seventeen years ago," Jaden says while moving around passenger vehicles.

"I feel like I'm floating, I don't feel any weight on my body. I like this a lot," Kim says.

"Are you down for this high speed quickie baby?" Jaden asks while steering the wheel left and right quickly.

"Yes!" She screams while leaning up to unzip Jaden's pants, "Just don't crash."

The Bugattee slows down as the top of the shield hits an overpass stripping away steel and concrete. Vehicles on the overpass feel a powerful vibration. The street begins to collapse onto the highway. Concrete and cars quickly fall down, hitting two of the UAVs flying at ground level behind the Bugattee. They explode and crash onto the highway. Vehicles on the highway slam on their brakes before the overpass.

Kim pulls her panties to the side and Jaden enters her. She slowly grinds and rides him, while her ass rubs the steering wheel gently. Intense pleasure circles their bodies.

A nanoscanner enters the car on its own and looks at Kim getting a ride on Jaden.

'AI, what are you doing? I need that nanoscanner to see behind and over me,' Jaden says.

'You are doing the same thing the couple a few days ago was doing on the highway. She is stuck on top of you and is trying to get up, but you won't let her.'

"You like that baby?" Kim asks.

'We are having sex, reproducing, remember?'

'Now? At a time like this? What is wrong with you humans?' AI asks.

"Yes, I do. That feels good," Jaden says to Kim while he curves himself inside of her again.

'I'm multi-tasking and relaxing. My huge headache is also going away. We are doing what Lois Lane and Superman wanted to do while they were flying in the air together,' Jaden says while chuckling and the nanoscanner goes back to over the Bugattee.

"Shit!" She yells while pulling down her bra and putting her breast in his face.

'You humans are very confusing sometimes. I can't understand this on a logical or creative prospective.'

'I'm doing the impossible AI. I have this superior feeling that I can do anything and no one can stop me,' Jaden says while sticking out his tongue to lick her nipples.

"I feel like I'm having sex with a blind man baby," she says in a sensual tone while momentarily stopping.

"You had sex with a blind man before?" Jaden asks while two more UAVs fly at ground level behind the Bugattee.

"No, silly, I'm just saying that this is probably how it might feel, because your eyes are completely closed," she says while continuing to ride him.

'Jaden the silent invasion has begun. In Europe, half of the population's minds went into neutral mode. Thousands are reported missing and it is spreading as it gets closer to the end of the countdown. I'm one hundred percent sure those missing humans are being beamed up to the mother ship,' AI says.

'Yeah, okay, AI.'

'Be careful, your Nanodrones are reporting you are getting close to overloading your brain. That is why you are getting headaches. Your neurons and cells are being overloaded with processing,' AI says.

'I will…will. I'm monitoring it.t.t…'

"What's this song?" Jaden asks, "I like it."

" 'Follow' by Incubus," she says while turning her head to look at the LCD screen. "It says *Halo 2 Soundtrack* on the screen."

"Nice," he says while reaching to turn up the fast paced rock and roll track.

"Damn baby! That's my spot again!" Kim yells and moans loudly while riding him faster.

The UAVs continue firing missiles and machine guns. The Bugattee slows down to 71 mph as the UAVs quickly pass by to circle back around. Twelve more UAVs and two Raptors approach from the north. There are several heavily armored tank drones about two miles ahead of the Bugattee blocking all the lanes on the highway. Jaden begins to concentrate on rotating the reverse shield outside of the forward shield. He is trying to create an electromagnetic pulse wave as AI suggested to him earlier. He concentrates heavily while Kim continues to ride on top of him. She is unaware of what is happening around her.

Both shields' rpm are moving in opposite directions at 120,000. The outside of the shield begins to glow bright. The Bugattee slows down to 42 mph and drives in the center lane of the highway.

'You need them both to reach 200,000 rpm,' AI says.

"I'm coming baby!" She yells while moaning very loudly.

Jaden is less than three-quarters of a mile from the tanks. The twenty-three total UAVs and Raptors all fire at the Bugattee at the same time. His body begins to tingle all around.

"Arrrggghh!" Jaden yells as he hits 201,000 rpm on both shields. Full shields go completely around the Bugattee as traction control comes up on the windshield.

"Aaahhhh!" Kim yells while the drums in the background to the music become louder.

There is a flash of bright yellow light exploding from the shields touching each other. An electromagnetic pulse wave moves in all directions, frying all electronic equipment as it passes. A few cars moving in the opposite direction turn off and slowly come to a stop. The missiles coming towards the Bugattee lose their thrust, but continue to cruise off course.

"Shit, shit shittt!" Kim screams while her body trembles all over.

Jaden moans and climaxes with her.

The UAVs and tank drones turn completely off. The UAVs fly out of control and towards the ground. They fall out of the air like flies all around the Bugattee. One of them lands directly in front of the Bugattee, but Jaden takes quick evasive action. Explosions and debris fly in different directions.

"What was that bright light and weird low throbbing sound?" Kim asks.

"Nothing much, just me releasing twice, one in you and one to anything electrical around us. Keep going, don't stop baby. I'm not finished yet," Jaden says while the full shield disappears from under the wheels.

"You came and you're still hard?" She asks.

"Yes, baby, I have the bionic stick," he says while she chuckles.

The two Raptor pilots manually eject. Jaden avoids UAVs crashing and exploding onto the highway around him. He quickly turns hard left using the reinforced shield around the front of the car to break through the concrete divider that splits north and south traffic. The car shakes as it crosses over, Kim tightens her grip around Jaden's neck. Kim continues to ride Jaden and make moaning sounds as she feels safe with him. The entire highway begins to explode as some missiles don't explode on impact. Fire and debris is exploding in all directions.

"Curve it baby, curve it into my spot. I want to feel that super orgasm again," Kim says while being more turned on by the sounds of fireworks exploding in the background. The Bugattee straightens up and drives north in the southbound HSCCV lane. The car quickly accelerates to 76 mph while just missing being hit by a falling F-22 Raptor exploding behind him. Her body floats up and down while the Bugattee's hard acceleration makes her breasts lean in Jaden's face. He sucks and licks her nipples with his tongue as Kim goes faster.

"Shit! Shit! Shit! Damn! Damn! Damn…Damn! Right there! Right there!" She screams while rubbing herself with her right index and middle finger.

The southbound traffic is stopped on the highway and people get out to look under the hoods of their cars. The Bugattee passes the tank drones on the right. They both climax at 125 mph.

"I love you baby," Kim whispers into Jaden's ear.

"I love you too, my sexy tasty Chinese food," he whispers back while they both giggle.

Very small, milky bubbles can be seen floating in the air around them.

WASHINGTON, D.C. PENTAGON 3:04 PM

"The terrorist anomaly survived and successfully took out our first wave of attack. The probability of two humans taking out a wave of UAV wolf pack drones is 0.1%. The EMI wave from the anomaly was highly unexpected. The technology the anomaly possesses must be obtained for our technological advances. Should we change strategy to try to capture the terrorist anomaly?" Motherdrone asks.

"No. Figure out a way to disrupt that high-energy source coming from space. Continue to set up a full double lane roadblock to destroy this threat. There is only so much luck one person can have, I'm sure it is running out. This threat must be annihilated at all cost. Setup a class A roadblock with titanium steel plates behind double the tank drones," Robinson says.

"Yes, I compute. My calculations conclude that using one UAV prototype Pegasus X-57 in full stealth mode will be the

91

best strategy. It has the experimental levitation engine and its advanced circuitry isn't affected by EMI waves," Motherdrone says.

"Yes, but that is a two billion dollar prototype experimental aircraft. We can't afford to have anything happen to it."

"Vice President Robinson. I will use the X-57 for surveillance only and only fire a shot if the opportunity arises. If there is an available shot to be taken, it won't get close to the anomaly. Local police have cleared the highway of passenger vehicles. There are only a few tractor-trailers left on the highway. I will run a second wave of UAVs and use nanotube titanium tank drones on both sides of the highway."

An officer walks into the small room with Robinson.

"The thermal imaging is ready for viewing, sir," the middle-aged officer says while images show up on the huge screen.

"Holy shit, that little cock sucker," Robinson says.

"Yes, sir, it is exactly what you are seeing. He was having sex with the female while he was driving. The energy shield protecting the car was being generated by the subject Jaden Marino and an outside energy coming from space. We were able to see thermal imaging when the shields would go off. The shield system is able to change into any shape very quickly. When the shield is on, you can see there are openings in the front of the car's shield. I'm assuming it is for air to circulate. There are also small holes in the rear where the air exits. The shield can also expand around the wheels, fully covering the vehicle when a missile or huge explosion occurs. The Bugattee doesn't have any traction on the road at such time. We also notice the energy shield getting very weak when the thermo bomb was dropped. The shield is not powerful enough to completely destroy nanotubing titanium steel. Setting up a full roadblock with snipers with thermo imaging gear is also an option," the officer says.

"Good work officer. I don't know if we will have time to deploy snipers," Robinson says while saluting the officer.

"Okay. By the way sir, the U.S. government in 2017 added a special government luxury tax on all vehicles over $100,000. The tax paid for all new vehicles to have a secret emergency Offstar car disabling feature installed."

"Good work officer. Get right on it!"

The officer salutes back and walks out of the room.

"Did the President land in Alaska yet?" Motherdrone asks.

"We are not sure, satellites have been down all around the northern hemisphere for the past twenty minutes. Radio transmissions aren't being received and we do not have any contact with Air Force 1."

"Should we launch an UAV search party?"

"No, I'm sure they are fine. That is for congress and the joint chiefs of staff to decide. You just concentrate your fifty billion dollar defense system to take out this terrorist threat."

"Yes, Vice President Robinson."

'Soon you will address me as President Robinson, Miss Motherdrone,' Robinson says to himself while chuckling.

FREDERICKSBURG, VA INTERSTATE I95 NORTH 3:13 PM

Kim is back in her seat with her clothes on. Vehicles are approaching the Bugattee as Jaden is still driving north in the southbound HSCCVL. He slows down and breaks through the concrete divider, back to the other side. They quickly accelerate on the north I-95 HSCCV lane.

The Bugattee's male voice begins to speak, "Offstar online, your vehicle will be disabled in one minute. Please pull over into a safe location."

"What is Offstar?" Jaden asks in a confused voice while looking at the countdown on the screen. He continues to drive around vehicles on the road at high speed.

Kim quickly replies, "We don't have Offstar installed in any of our vehicles. The Offstar services offer live location information, calls authorities if someone is in an accident, helps investigators in accidents and tracks and disables stolen cars for police. The government bought the private company out in 2016 and there have been reports of the government listening in on people's conversations, even when the service wasn't on. The government must have secretly begun putting it in everyone's vehicles. That means this car probably has a vehicle black box."

Jaden interrupts, "How does it receive the signals? How can I stop the car from being disabled?"

"It uses a satellite to send the final disabling signal," Kim quickly says.

Thirty seconds continue to countdown and Jaden accelerates.

"I can block the signal with the full shields right?" Jaden asks.

"Yes, but the satellite sends out disabling signals for up to thirty minutes."

"Shit, I can't drive without any traction on the ground, nor can I keep the shields up for thirty minutes," Jaden says with his hand on his chin.

"Ten, nine, eight…." The vehicle says.

'AI, I need you to locate that satellite above us.'

'Yes sir, I'm locating it now with the Gravhawk's nanoscanners and scanning for microwaves transmitting signals.'

"Three, two, one…."

Jaden activates the full shield around the Bugattee. The microwave signal from the satellite travels towards Earth and hits the outside of the shield in an attempt to disable the car. Jaden can actually see the satellite signal hitting the top of the shield. The wheels lose traction to the ground. Zero traction flashes on the windshield. The signals keep coming down.

"The signals don't stop until the vehicle responds to confirm the engines are off," Kim says.

The car slows down to 25 mph in the HSSCVL. One UAV comes out of nowhere and fires a missile at the Bugattee. It is a direct hit and the force from the missile passes through the shield and spins the car into 360° circles. Jaden tries to steer, but he doesn't have any control. Kim closes her eyes and braces herself. The vehicle stops completely on the highway with fire still burning on the outside. A light pole falls directly onto the Bugattee from the left. The pole splits into two pieces and a crashing sound proceeds.

She mumbles and says in a quick, nervous voice, "In the summer of 2015, the sun had strong solar wind storms that temporarily and permanently destroyed satellites. If you can recreate the same effect, it might be easier to disable it and the signals."

"Thanks baby," Jaden says.

'I found the satellite orbiting in high orbit. There is a lot of debris in low and high orbit...' AI says.

'Yeah yeah, AI, not now. You heard Kim right?'

'Yes, I heard her distorted speaking.'

'Do you think that might work?'

'Yes, I can easily divert the sun's solar winds outside the magnetosphere into a concentrated beam at the satellite transmitting towards your location.'

The Bugattee sits on the highway backwards with smoke coming from around it.

"This is for putting car thieves on the unemployment line Spystar!" Jaden yells.

"Yeah, this is for spying and listening in on millions of people's private conversations!" Kim yells.

Concentrated solar flare energy hits the satellite directly, frying its microchips and then exploding it. The microwave signals stop bombarding the Bugattee. The rear wheels touch the ground and Jaden puts the car into reverse. He quickly accelerates backwards, then turns the wheel and shifts it into drive. They continue to drive on the highway and Kim opens her eyes.

'Would you like me to destroy some space junk in orbit, while I'm up here?' AI asks.

'Don't waste your time, if the Darclonians take over humans, I'm sure they could clean it up faster than humans,' Jaden snaps.

A few minutes pass by.

"It's amazing how certain things from your memory are in so many random places, Kim."

"I know. I'm surprised so many of my memories are implanted in your mind and vice versa. I randomly remember things from your childhood," she says.

"Can you check my e-mail on the Internet baby. I want to see if James e-mailed me," he says.

"Sure," she says while touching areas on the passenger side windshield with two fingers and moving things around.

Jaden gives her his login information that AI setup at the hospital for him.

'Jaden, I would suggest only keeping this high energy coming down towards you for another ten minutes or less. The low radiation levels are getting higher around Kim. Also, this high energy trail can be detected by your government and the Darclonians.'

'I understand, can you stop the feed now and continue later?' Jaden asks.

'Yes, but it might take a little time to lock on again. Those UAV drones are very synchronized and are all being controlled by one source. They also inflict the most damage on your shield system. I followed and trailed their signal source. There is a government blimp about 72,000 feet above you. The huge airship is receiving a laser signal from several spread out satellites. The blimp is using microwaves and radio waves to communicate instantly with the UAV drones, tank drones and all video cameras on the highway.'

'Interesting, I bet there is no delay at that high speed. We need to take out that blimp. I can't reach it that high up, but maybe there is something you can do. Can you put the energy path through the blimp?' Jaden asks.

'It isn't the type of energy that will destroy a blimp. An explosive type of energy would be needed,' AI says.

'Can you shoot a torpedo from where you are in the North Pole?'

'That is possible. But it would have to be a long-range torpedo, so it could change directions. I wouldn't want the government to know my location.'

'Okay, get on it.'

'Yes sir.'

"Baby, you have an e-mail here from two people," Kim says while tapping the windshield and sliding her fingers over different areas on it.

There are no UAVs flying in a five-mile circumference. There are also barely any cars on the road, except a few tractor-trailers miles ahead.

"There is an e-mail from James. It reads: Hey man! Jaden is that really you man? I thought you were dead. When I saw a message from you on Myfacebook, I couldn't believe my eyes. Where you been the last eighteen years? Guess what man? I'm a millionaire now. I won the lottery twice in a row. Call me at 516-555-9089 my old friend."

"Call him for me baby," Jaden says.

"I'll text him first," Kim says.

"Text? What is wrong with an old fashion telephone call?" Jaden asks.

"People barely talk on the phone now, everything is about instant message, brain text, computer phone text and vehicle text. Some people actual talk into a microphone and the software translates the voice into words to be instant messaged," Kim says while dialing numbers on the phone.

"That is crazy, what is the point of doing all of that?" Jaden asks.

"I don't know, this is the norm. The number went to voice mail," Kim says while handing Jaden the phone.

Jaden takes the phone and speaks into it, "Hey, James, it is your old best friend Jaden. I have a long story to tell. Congratulations on winning the lottery man, I knew great things would happen to you. I have an emergency situation happening in Manhattan. I want to know if you could meet me there. Around midtown or lower Manhattan would be good. I can't talk much over the phone, but I'm going to need your help. Text, call or e-mail back if you can. See you there man," Jaden says while giving Kim the phone back. Kim hangs up and tries to redial her father's cell, but it goes to voice mail again.

"The second e-mail is from a General Peters, it reads: Jaden Marino, I know you are here to help us. I'm aware of the pending attack against America and the world. Vice President Robinson has completely lost it and is trying to kill you at all cost. You are on the top of the terrorist kill list. I believe he has something to do with the President's airplane being non-responsive. We have lost all communications with it over north Canada. Radar is showing it is on autopilot and flying at Mach 2.5 at these coordinates.... We believe no one onboard had a special helmet that would have protected them from these unknown energy waves coming from space. Air Force 1 will run out of gas in the next hour and crash. We have attempted an air board without success. Marshal Lopez told us how you saved Flight 104 on Saturday. The Panstarr telescope has detected something sitting between Earth and the moon. We desperately need your help. If you are still alive and getting this, call me at 202-555-5131. That is a secured line. President Paylin was never aware of these facts about you. Her life desperately needs to be spared if we plan to fight this alien invasion together. If she dies, Robinson will be President of the United States," Kim reads.

"Wow, that's deep. Let the conspiracies begin," Jaden says.

"Do you believe him?" Kim asks.

"No, not really. It's probably a trap, I don't trust anyone in the government now. But save the number, I'm going to have AI check into that Air Force 1 situation. Rescuing my daughter is first priority. I'll call him if the story checks out," Jaden says.

'Earth calling AI. Pick up AI. Nanu, Nanu,' Jaden says.

'Nanu? Nanu?' AI asks.

'It was from the television show *Mork and Mindy* from the eighties. Oh, forget it. You don't remember much from my memory huh?' Jaden asks.

'I only remember relevant things. I'm ready to fire the special torpedo,' AI says.

'Hold on a second, don't fire the torpedo yet...' Jaden says while explaining to AI the situation with Air Force 1. AI sends a high-speed nanoscanner and nanoeye towards the direction of north Alaska. They scan the entire area for thousands of miles in seconds. AI finds Air Force 1 flying at 1862 mph.

'I forgot you don't have to connect the Gravhawk's nanoscanners together,' Jaden says.

The nanoeye looks at the passengers on board; all are unconscious. The video images are being sent back to the Gravhawk and relays through the planet to Jaden.

"Kim, can you tell me if you see the President onboard?" Jaden asks while putting his right hand over her eyes.

The nanoeye quickly sees secret service men in suits and the President's cabinet people laying unconscious all around the airplane. Kim sees President Stefanie Paylin behind a desk lying on the floor with her family pictures in her arms.

"Oh no, the President is laid out and unconscious," Kim says nervously. "Why can't I control this nanoscanner?"

"You can't manually control this one, it is the Gravhawk's nanoeye, AI is controlling it. Why would you want to control? Hey! Wait a second, I just read that dirty thought that just flashed in your frontal lobe," Jaden says.

The Bugattee is moving on the highway at the speed limit as it passes tractor-trailers in the left lane. The windmill blades on the rear continue to spin. They pass a sign that says the next exit is twelve miles.

"You wanted to see what kind of panties the President wears?" Jaden asks.

"No I didn't... Where did you get that from?" She asks modestly.

"You are a twisted individual. Why would you want to do that?" Jaden asks.

"Okay, you caught me. I was just curious, what the President of the United States wore under the business skirt, nothing more," Kim explains.

"Yeah, yeah, okay Dr. Freak. I remember your experimental college days," Jaden says while removing his hand from her eyes.

'I thought I was bad,' Jaden says to AI.

"I'll show you a freak," Kim says while grabbing Jaden's right hand and sucks on his fingers in her mouth.

'You two were made for each other,' AI says.

'Tell me about it.'

Two state trooper cars come on the entrance ramp to get on the highway and speed up with their sirens on.

'AI, it is multi-tasking time. You have the Gravhawk's fast computer processing and your own computer processing. I need you to land Air Force 1 the same way we did on Flight 104. I'm also going to need you to take out that blimp with the torpedo.'

'I don't know if it's possible to land Air Force 1 from here. They don't have enough fuel and they are too far from an airport. But I will try my best,' AI says.

'I'm also going to need you to stand by on locking on to me again. I might need that high energy surge soon,' Jaden says.

'Yes sir. I'm preparing a long-range pink torpedo. This should be strong enough to destroy the blimp. Your government would call this an ice to water, water to air, air to space, space to air missile.'

The Bugattee speeds up as it passes more trucks. A nanoscanner detects a full roadblock two miles ahead. There is a row of tank drones completely covering the southbound and northbound routes. The nanoscanner detects high magnetically charged energy in the rail gun tank cannons. There is also a two-foot deep carbon titanium steel bar coming one and a half feet from the highway. Jaden also notices something flying invisibly one hundred feet above him. A nanoscanner quickly moves towards the unknown object and scans it.

"Top-secret government X-57 prototype? Ever heard of that, Kim?" Jaden asks.

"No, baby."

"There is something flying above us semi-invisible with reflective materials and it is flying using a strange engine to produce magnetic propulsion. The nanoscanner is detecting opaque body materials. The aircraft has two missiles that have kinetic energy compounds," Jaden says.

"Interesting…be careful. The government is sneaky with their secret weapons. I still can't reach my father."

'AI, what will I need to go through the roadblock?' Jaden asks.

'The shields aren't strong enough to break though the titanium tanks and steel blockage,' AI says.

'Shit, I'll figure something out,' he says.

AI fires the pink torpedo from under seventy-five feet of ice and water from the North Pole. The torpedo has pink particles moving on the outside of it and contains billions of nanobots. It breaks through the ice, changes directions and flies south twenty feet over land. AI also starts to work on remote controlling the pilot of Air Force 1.

Two tractor-trailer drivers are talking on their radios to each other as they see the Bugattee in their rearview mirrors, quickly approaching them with the police following. They stop following behind each other in the middle lane and each drive on the broken white lines, blocking all three lanes. The truck on the left is aqua blue with advertisements of getting your free carbon footprint. The truck on the right is grey and white. Jaden sees this blockage in all three lanes and slows down behind them as they block the highway. The police quickly catch up. Jaden honks the horn repeatedly behind the huge trucks swerving back and forth. Kim closes her eyes and puts her hands over her face.

"Shit, these bastards are blocking me in," Jaden says.

"I don't want to see, I'm scared of big trucks on the highway," Kim says.

"You aren't scared of big trucks. Come on, what about that time back in May 2015, when the 18-wheeler driver cut you off on the highway and he poured coffee from his window onto your windshield?" Jaden asks while looking at her with her hands over her face. "You drove in front of him and tossed a 32 oz Slurpee into the air through your sunroof and it landed on his windshield. Then you quickly drove off with your middle finger through the sunroof."

"That was an exception; I had my period then and I wasn't taking any shit from anyone. I keep forgetting you can remember events in my past. I'm still trying to get used to this. I'm amazed you know so much about me."

"I love the fire deep inside of you," Jaden says.

The Bugattee slows down to 47 mph.

"Please stop your vehicle you have nowhere to go," the troopers in the police car say over a loudspeaker.

Meanwhile the pink torpedo is quickly accelerating south across the sky at high speed looking like a bright meteor.

The roadblock is approaching in half a mile. The Bugattee tries to accelerate in the HSCCV lane, but the left truck swerves over there also, blocking off the Bugattee. Jaden slows down behind them. The military is telling the troopers and the truck drivers to stand down.

"We have this little prick in the sports car cut off, he isn't getting by us," the truck driver on the left says over his radio.

"We will be forced to open fire on you," the troopers say to the Bugattee.

"I have an idea Kim, but I'm going to need your help," Jaden says while Kim takes her hands from over her eyes.

"The truck on the left doesn't have any cargo in its trailer. I need you to find the manual for this car and tell me the weight of it," Jaden says.

Kim quickly opens the small glove compartment and finds the manual. Jaden creates a 440,000-rpm shield around the Bugattee. Anti-gravity Nanodrones are over the hood of the

Bugattee. He speeds up to the left side of the blue tractor-trailer. Kim looks down flipping through the manual. He slows down where the double rear wheels on the trailer meet, as the truck tries to cut him off. Jaden slowly turns right into the huge rear wheels and the outside shield slowly destroys the rubber and iron in the huge wheels. The rear trailer slowly drops to the ground as the Bugattee slows down. Debris and metal roll across the highway.

The trailer's rear drags on the ground creating bright sparks and a loud grinding and scraping sound floods the airwaves. The truck continues to drive while the rear doors open and break against the highway. The Bugattee swerves around the two doors spinning on the ground. Jaden can see the roadblock ahead with his eyes. The tank drones are pointing their 20mm rail guns at the Bugattee from both sides of the highway. Jaden does calculations in his brain as he slows down again.

"You know Kim, in high school we always wondered why we need to learn calculus if we would never use it in life. Today I'm using all those calculations I used to do on a graphing calculator, but in my head," Jaden says while the Bugattee stops completely in the middle lane.

"You should thank your math teacher one of these days," she says while flipping through the pages of the manual.

"Turn off your engine and step out of the car with your hands up," a state trooper twenty feet behind the Bugattee says over a microphone.

"I think I will do that when all of this is done. I used to hate calculus with all the stupid formulas and equations that I would never use. Now it all makes sense, especially with this equation solution I'm working on now," Jaden says.

"What are you calculating?" She asks.

"You'll see. Do you have the curb weight of this car?"

"Not yet, I think it might be easier if I looked it up on the Internet," Kim says while touching the passenger side windshield. She looks ahead and gets an idea of what is about to happen.

Two state troopers get out of their vehicles with their guns drawn and approach the Bugattee. The two trucks slow down to 5 mph as they see the police are walking up on the Bugattee.

"Got it! 2212 lbs" Kim yells.

"Damn, that was fast. Okay, so that is 2487 lbs with our weight…" he says. "Hold on baby!"

Jaden presses the button to open the convertible top as he unbuttons his seat belt. Jaden floors the pedal and the tires skid off. The troopers open fire at the tires, but the bullets miss. Jaden is concentrating and multi-tasking on many things as the percentage usage of his brain increases past eighty percent. The engines quickly change gears. Kim covers her eyes with both of her hands. The Bugattee is aiming straight for the rear of the trailer still dragging on the ground. The top roof slowly moves to the rear, as the Bugattee reaches 65 mph. Jaden sends out invisible impulses from the shield to mess with the aiming of the tank drones. The tank drones begin firing at the car. Small impulses of electromagnetic energy move out in all directions from the tank drones. It affects the engines and electronics in the tractor-trailers. Hot magnetically charged steel projectiles propel down the nozzle of the tanks simultaneously. They exit the nozzle at 8900 mph in the direction of the Bugattee and quickly heat up as they push through the air. They look like blurry flashes of yellow light. Jaden's mind goes into nanotime 100x, as the projectiles move slower in a blur. He narrowly misses being hit by one. The front of the car reaches the rear of the tractor-trailer. The Bugattee tilts upwards and drives up the rear of the empty trailer while projectiles make huge holes throughout the steel hull. Projectiles bombard the tractor-trailer and pass through it like paper. The drivers of the trucks die as their bodies rip apart. The tractor-trailer on the right slows down and crashes into the shoulder. The one Jaden is driving in continues forward. Kim grunts with the blunt force of the car changing directions upwards. Jaden concentrates most of his shield energy around the front of the car, while the reverse shield is quickly moving over the forward. On the ground, a white circle of smoke is about 500 feet around the area. The Nanodrones concentrate their energy at the front of the energy shield. The front of the car penetrates the metal front frame of the trailer at 77 mph, creating a huge hole in it. The Bugattee goes airborne as the tractor-trailer is slowly engulfed in flames.

"Nice!" Jaden very quickly yells out loud.

Jaden enhances the anti-gravity Nanodrones around the car. The X-57 aircraft fires an abnormal looking missile towards the airborne Bugattee. The wheels are spinning in midair as debris is flying in different directions. A projectile hits the rear of the shield areas and passes through several layers and narrowly misses a windmill blade. The force from the blunt strike makes the Bugattee slowly spin counterclockwise.

The airborne car ascends over the beginning of the roadblock at an altitude of thirty-five feet. Swooshing sounds pass by the car from the yellow glowing projectiles. The nanoscanners detect burning metal in the area. The two opposite directional shields touch each other creating an EMI in all directions. A bright light flashes in all directions as hot fire still burns around the shield. The tank drones stop firing their rail gun cannons. The unaffected missile continues towards the Bugattee. The kinetic missile hits the rear shield area of the Bugattee. The powerful force passes through the Bugattee, causing it to quickly rotate in the opposite clockwise direct. The kinetic missile is eating the shield generating Nanodrones. Fire is all around the full energy shields. The Bugattee's convertible top is fully open and fire is all over him. Kim feels the brunt impact and begins to scream. Her slow sounding scream sounds like a man's deep voice to Jaden. Her body briefly jitters towards him from the impact, hugging her body against the seat belt.

The outside shield absorbs the powerful explosion, but loses eighty percent of its rpm speed. The Bugattee continues to spins out of control at a high speed. Sounds of spinning wheels echo in all directions. Another bigger missile is shot towards the car as the X-57 aircraft levitates not too far behind the car. Jaden holds onto the steering wheel while kneeling in the seat and quickly turning to his left. Jaden is standing up, but slightly crouching with his left leg bent on his seat and his right leg is on the floor, leaning against the steering wheel. Pro-gravity Nanodrones in Jaden's feet are keeping him from floating away from the Bugattee. He sees debris slowly flying in different directions around him. Jaden stops creating the shield around the vehicle. A trail of white smoke tunnels up from the ground and up into the bottom of the car. The bigger missile gets within twelve feet of the Bugattee. The rear of the car slowly spins around to face the opposite direction as Jaden's mind is in 50x nanotime. Jaden brings both hands toward his shoulders. His brain is at eighty-nine percent usage and his brain waves begin to spike making him feel tremendous pain. Jaden's nervous system feels the effects as he keeps the timer on nanotime continuing to extend. He surpasses his nanotime limit and his brain feels the damaging effects.

Jaden sees the semi-invisible X-57 and missile slowly getting into sight from the spinning. He extends both arms and fires a gravity shock wave and atoms ripper towards the kinetic missile. The energy leaves his body. The missile is hit by the powerful gravity shock wave and atoms ripper weapon. Portions of the missile instantly disintegrate and there is a small explosion as the forces quickly move towards the X-57. The Bugattee begins to descend towards the ground as the anti-gravity Nanodrones begin to strongly disrupt the gravity under the car. He focuses most of his concentration on that since he feels the car quickly falling towards the ground. The X-57 is caught in the shock wave and propels backwards at a fast speed. Jaden sits back down in the driver's seat as his nanotime goes off. The Bugattee continues to float and spin closer towards the highway.

Jaden puts the gearshift into reverse and presses on the gas. He straightens out the wheels as the car gently lands backwards on the highway at a momentum speed of 42 mph. Skidding sounds are heard as the car hits the ground. The car touches down like an airplane and the shocks absorb the lighter car. The windshield displays electricity coming from the shocks of the car to help charge the battery system. The Bugattee continues driving backwards on the highway. Jaden holds his head as he feels pain in different areas.

"Are we alive?" Kim asks.

"Yes baby," Jaden grunts.

"I can't keep doing this Jaden. This is wrecking my nerves now," she says.

"Me either, this is wrecking my brain cells and giving me a migraine super headache," Jaden snaps while groaning.

"I feel so dizzy from all that spinning around. Why are we driving backwards?"

"Oh yeah, let me fix that backwards thing. I was practicing my driving backwards skills," he says.

He slams on the brakes while turning the steering wheel to the right. The car whips to the left and he puts the gear into neutral and then drive. The wheels peel off as he hits the accelerator.

"I thought the Dukes of Hazards, Knight Rider jump and James Bond action sequence you just experienced would be a turn on for you," Jaden says.

"I had my eyes mostly closed, I was too scared to look."

"Would you like a replay of it? I had the nanoscanner recording it from different angles like movie cameras," he says.

"Sure," she says while she grabs his right hand and places it over her eyes.

The debris from the missile and X-57 land in a lake a few miles away off the highway. Kim sees the video replaying through her eyes in slow motion.

'AI, are you there?' Jaden asks while continuing to drive high speed with one hand.

'Yes, I'm here.'

'I'm going to need that high energy surge soon, my energy is at twenty percent. That kinetic missile drained a lot of my shield energy and destroyed some Nanodrones,' Jaden says.

'Okay, I'm working on locking onto you again now. I noticed that many parts of the X-57 were made with technology not from Earth. The pink torpedo was destroyed by your government's air defense system. Lasers were fired from the ground and anti-air missiles took out the torpedo at the same time. The blimp is still online and is intercepting all of the communications. I'm going to fire an artificial intelligence black torpedo nanite-sphere, it will hit the blimp guaranteed.'

Kim removes Jaden's hands from her eyes.

"Wow baby! You just pulled off the almost impossible. That high-speed jump through the back of the tractor-trailer in the Bugattee was unbelievable. It was like watching a Michael Bay movie, but ten times the special effects. I like how the nanoscanner passed through the explosion to change angles, while the wheels were spinning in slow motion. The missile explosion outside the shield created a nice lighting effect. The gravity shock wave was the icing on the cake. Very cool, baby," Kim says while looking at him smiling.

"I'm glad you liked it. I told you it was awesome. I'm sure I broke some kind of world record. I feel like an unstoppable legend," he says.

'How is Air Force 1 coming along?' Jaden asks.

'I'm still trying to get full control of it and there isn't enough fuel for it to land at the nearby airport in Alaska. The aircraft is 190 miles north of Alaska, over the Arctic Ocean. The craft is at 23,000 feet and at 1091 mph. I'll try to figure out something. Five minutes ago, two hypersonic UAV drones successfully dropped off two SWATbots onto the hull of Air Force 1 when I was trying to get control of the pilot. But the aircraft was moving at Mach 3 and the SWATbots couldn't hold on. They fell off and parachuted down towards the ocean. This doesn't make sense, why would they fly into an area full of Darclonian proton energy area without any protection around their brains?'

'I smell a full government conspiracy. Shit, I see another reinforced full roadblock being created 2.1 miles ahead of me with more tank drones. This is the last roadblock before the highway splits off. The government just doesn't give up,' Jaden says.

'I don't know how you going to make it through the roadblock. I'm doing high speed calculations as we speak,' AI says.

'There has to be a way. I want to ram straight through it at a high speed,' Jaden says.

'For you to ram through the reinforced titanium tanks and nanotubing solid steel bar behind the tanks, you would need a outside shield speed of one million rpm minimum and the help of matrix vortex particles. I can transmit some of those particles through your nanoscanners from space. The only thing is that it is going to be near impossible for you to get the shield's rpm at 1,000,000 by yourself. Just trying to get to that speed will really overload your organic brain. Even with the help of the Nanodrones in your brain's neurons, it still won't help. We need to figure out another way, it is too dangerous,' AI says.

'There isn't another way. I'm going to have to do this, I know I can do this. I have confidence that I can do this or anything.'

'This isn't a superhero movie, where special effects save the hero. You can seriously injury your brain, give yourself a seizure and put yourself into a coma. Not to mention killing yourself and Kim in a huge fireball if you don't reach that minimum rpm,' AI says.

'I don't have a choice, I'm going to go for it. I know I can handle this.'

'Yes sir.'

"Kim, play some good music for me, I need to concentrate on this last roadblock."

Kim changes the radio station to Cinemagic.

"What kind of music is this?" He asks.

"These are movie soundtrack songs. It is cool and something I'm sure you would like. It always helped me to relax and concentrate," she says.

"Cool, I'm open to something different."

Jaden stops in the middle lane of the I-95 highway. The convertible roof closes back and there are no cars or vehicles on the highway in both directions. The roadblock is 1.6 miles in front of the Bugattee. The _Dark Knight_ soundtrack song number twelve begins to play. He stares down the road of life or death. Jaden has his right hand over the gear shifter in manual mode. He shifts the gear and steps on the accelerator pedal. Kim raises the volume and Jaden focuses on his energy shield's rpm moving around the Bugattee. He concentrates on the energy particles and Nanodrones moving around the car faster and faster. AI locks onto Jaden's nanoscanners above the Bugattee. The weapon energy beams down to him with some matrix vortex particles. His weapons energy goes up to one hundred percent. Kim begins to hear a humming sound as the shield's rpm reaches 722,000. The shield glows around the car. His breathing increases and blood pressure quickly rises. The Bugattee accelerates to 99 mph. Jaden's eyes are glowing blue as they are focusing on the matrix vortex shield slowly forming blue lightning in front of the car. The shield energy is duplicating itself by forming light energy patterns in front of the Bugattee. His brain feels a huge amount of pain in different areas. The pain spreads around his body. His body begins to shake uncontrollably as the roadblock quickly approaches. Shiny black material begins to cover Jaden's fingers and hands. His rpm reaches 870,091. Kim closes her eyes as her heart quickly beats. She takes a deep breath as the outside shield begins to glow with a blue tint. Jaden's brain usage reaches ninety-six percent as his brain waves are spiking. The shiny black material slowly dissolves some of the steering wheel. The plastic on top of the gearshift disappears. Jaden lifts his hands off those two areas and holds his hands in front of him.

"Kim, hold the steering wheel straight for me. My hands are covered in this black shit," Jaden quickly says.

"Okay," she says and holds the steering wheel. "Are you okay baby? Your body trembling isn't a good sign."

"I'm fine, just need to concentrate," he says in a trembling voice.

Blood comes down his nose and his brain is glowing under his scalp. The theme music picks up tempo as his speed picks up to 141 mph. Huge 105mm saber cannon shells, rockets and thousands of bullets a second are shot simultaneously from eight tank drones on both sides of the highway. Jaden's blood pressure continues to rise. Very loud cannon fire take over the airwaves as fire and explosions ignite around the blue-tinted shield of the Bugattee. The car feels the brunt of the explosions as Kim's left hand shudders on the steering wheel. Jaden sees the rpm speed reaching 918,000 and his brain usage is at one hundred percent. There are warning signs on his eye screen. His brain begins to spike as his body continues to shake uncontrollably. The outside shield is glowing brighter blue. The area in front of the shield is consuming the explosions and high-speed projectiles. Kim squints from all of the bright lights and explosions.

Sweat is running down his face and he breathes very heavily. The front shields take on maximum projectiles. His brain spikes at 110% usage as he reaches 1,009,421 rpm. The front of the Bugattee rams through roadblock at 175 mph and there is a huge explosion. The enhanced front shield area instantly disintegrates the tank drones and steel metal bar coming from the highway. The engines begin to shutter as three of them turn off. A huge fireball of smoke spins upwards into the sky. The tank drones on the southbound side of the highway continue to fire towards the fast moving, glowing Bugattee. Thirty seconds pass by and Jaden's foot comes off the accelerator as the car begins to slow down. Kim keeps her hand on the steering wheel. The shield around the car disappears.

COMPUTER GEAR CONTROL ERROR flashes on the Bugattee's LCD screen.

His body continues to shakes violently and uncontrollably. Jaden blacks out. Spit and drool comes from his mouth. His nose bleeds and the mysterious black material disappears from his hands. His head slumps over like a sleeping drunk person.

"Jaden, are you okay?" Kim asks while she has her right hand on the steering wheel and turning to watch the road.

There is no response and his body stops shaking. His eyes roll back into his head. AI rides the last energy wave beam from space towards Jaden.

"Jaden! Jaden! Wake up!" Kim yells while the Bugattee cruises at 25 mph.

She lowers the volume and touches Jaden to wake up. She can't reach the brake pedal to stop the car, so she puts the gear shifter into neutral and turns the steering wheel to the right onto the shoulder. The car slows down and Kim shifts the Bugattee into park. The vehicle jerks forward and Jaden's head hits the steering wheel.

"Jaden, baby…" she says while taking his pulse on his hand and neck.

She feels that he has a pulse, but he is not breathing. His head and neck jerk for a few seconds as AI enters his body. She sees that he isn't breathing.

"Jaden! Baby, are you back?" She asks while looking around the deserted highway.

'Jaden!' AI yells. 'What a mess in here. There are millions of brain cells damaged and structural damage to the cerebellum,' AI says.

Kim opens the passenger door and runs to the driver's side. She opens the door and pulls Jaden out by his shoulder onto the ground. She begins to administer CPR on him. She breathes into his mouth and pushes on his chest as he lays unconscious.

The Nanodrones are already trying to repair damaged brain cells, tissue and nerve cells. Jaden's mind is in a full vegetable state coma. Kim continues to administer CPR on Jaden.

'Kim, he is getting oxygen through his pores! There isn't anything you can do for him right now…. I forgot, she can't hear me. Think, AI, think; Think creatively. How can I communicate with Kim?' AI asks himself.

WASHINGTON, D.C. PENTAGON 3:39 PM

"Object and anomalies are still alive, Vice President. Estimated total damage for tank drones, UAV drones, highway structures, possible civilian lawsuits…." Motherdrone says.

"I don't care about the…" Robinson says.

"….twenty-two billion dollars…"

"… damage costs, tell me our options now and the status of the unknown bogie projectile."

"The UAVs and tank drones so far are not effective against the subject. There aren't any more UAVs or tank drones in the area at the time. Congress had an emergency

113

session five minutes ago and they have limited your access for using live military personnel. I came up with another strategy, as you can see from the screens the subject seems to be injured. We can do a silent attack using the special forces prototype exoskeleton nanobond fifth generation kangaroo body suits."

"Good idea, we can run live tests on those million dollar each exoskeleton suits. I'm also glad the X-57 wasn't badly damaged and can be recovered," Robinson says.

"The black sphere projectile has been unstoppable so far. It originated from the North Pole. Ground to air lasers has had no effect on it. It elevated into space and disabled one of our satellites. It has reprogrammed three of our air-to-air missiles while it was on its way down. Its trajectory is heading down towards the blimp over Virginia. Three of our missiles are following this projectile to destroy our own airship. The blimp's communications are temporarily offline and it is slowly moving its location. The projectile will hit our communication blimp in four minutes. The special forces soldiers are being deployed as we speak, " Motherdrone says.

"Even if the blimp is destroyed we have backup blimps and we will know the location of the UFO if it fired another projectile," Motherdrone says.

WOODBRIDGE, VA I-95 NORTHBOUND SHOULDER 3:43 PM

Jaden is laid out on the ground and Kim continues to give him CPR while she is on her knees over him. His heart is still beating and he has a low pulse. AI comes up with an idea. There is a loud explosion echoing down from the sky sounding like thunder. The airship at 70,000 feet explodes in the sky.

AI speaks to himself and unconscious Jaden, 'Your involuntary muscles aren't working. I can't control or remote into your body manually, that will cause permanent damage in your motor cortex part of your brain. I need to keep oxygen in your lungs so I can talk out of your windpipes in your throat, so I can get a message to Kim. But she keeps pushing the oxygen out. Okay, I'll hold your lung muscles next time she breathes in.'

"You can't die on me, baby. Not now, I need you, and I love you," Kim pleads while breathing into his mouth and tears are running down her face. The warm tears land on Jaden's unconscious face.

Kim remembers what Jaden's father used to tell him in karate school when he was young. A slow moving military propeller aircraft flies towards Jaden and Kim from a distance. On fire fragments of the blimp showers around the area.

"Wake up! Get up! You're no quitter, you are a fighter. Don't quit on me now. Tuck in the pain and stand up like a soldier!" Kim yells while pushing on his chest. She stops when she feels his lung muscles hold in the air.

Jaden whispers in a mumbling voice with his eyes closed, "...radio... car.... FM"

"What? What did you say baby?" She asks.

She puts her right ear over his mouth. Jaden's lungs take another breath and AI uses his vocal cords and tongue.

'You bit your tongue in a few places, Jaden you jerk,' AI says to Jaden.

"Kimmm, this is A...I. Turn... on... the...FM radio...stat-ion....in... the car," Jaden's mouth says.

"Okay," she says while quickly standing up and sitting in the driver's seat accessing the radio.

She comes back out of the vehicle and kneels over Jaden.

"Okay, AI I turned the radio to 87.1, now what?" She asks.

"Kim can you hear me?" AI says through the speakers in the Bugattee.

She jumps up from the loud voice and it scares her.

"Yes, I can. What has happened to Jaden? Is he okay?" She asks while holding her chest.

"He is in a deep coma. His brain and nerve cells suffered damage in a few areas in his brain. He suffered a seizure when he overused his brain. Don't worry about him not breathing, Nanodrones are filtering air directly into his bloodstream. His vitals are identical and normal to a patient in a coma. Nanodrones are looking for him now in his subconscious," AI says.

"What can I do?" She asks.

"We need to…" AI is interrupted.

"We need to what?" She asks.

"The nanoscanners are detecting something. There is a hovering, two foot round, white, donut-shaped UAV spy chopper 300 feet directly over us, watching us with a small camera. A military propeller aircraft has dropped off two military men and a female officer in exotic exoskeleton suits. They are parachuting towards the ground about 1.5 miles behind us. The small camera's signal is splitting towards the military men," AI says while the propeller aircraft passes over them at 5300 feet and keeps going.

"Shit, that isn't good," Kim says while sniffling and looking up towards the aircraft flying over her, "I don't see anything except the aircraft above."

"They are using opaque materials, they are semi-invisible. It is very hard to see with human eyes. Trust me they are there and they just landed. They just began running towards us. Something is extending out of their feet and they are getting taller. They are running and leaping six feet into the air. We need to get Jaden into the passenger seat and you need to drive right away," AI says.

"They are using bionic boots, I read about those. They are banned for civilians. We have to hurry, those boots allow soldiers to run around 25 mph," Kim says while grabbing Jaden under the shoulders. She drags him around the rear of the Bugattee as she hears sounds from exhaust of the muffler.

"They aren't boots, they are built into their exoskeleton suits like small shoes. Correction, they are leaping at 41 mph towards us," AI says.

Another special forces man in an exoskeleton suit jumps out of the aircraft. He has a small sniper gun on his back. Kim tries to lift Jaden into the passenger seat, but she can't.

"I can't lift him. I'm not strong enough," Kim says while continuing to try to lift Jaden's lifeless body.

"Why not?" AI asks.

"I'm a small woman and I'm only 115 lbs," Kim says while breathing heavily trying to lift him.

"Can't a woman do everything a man can?" AI asks.

"That is a metaphor. This isn't the time. I'm a human girl, AI, not a Terminator robot. Is there any way you can do to help me lift him?" She asks.

The kangaroo leaping semi-invisible soldiers get within half a mile behind Kim and Jaden. The female soldier is in front and they wear serious faces under their suits. One soldier two miles in front of the Bugattee lands on the ground and he gets rid of his parachute.

"I have an idea," AI says.

"Hurry, I hear low clicking sounds approaching," Kim says.

"They are 500 feet behind us, lift him now," AI says through the car speakers.

Kim lifts Jaden easily into the passenger seat.

"What the hell? How did you do that?" She asks while placing his legs into the vehicle and closes the door.

She runs around to the driver's seat, climbs in and closes the vertical door.

"I used anti-gravity Nanodrones around his body to reduce his weight by seventy-five percent. Hurry and drive, they are almost at the vehicle," AI says in 10.1 Dolby stereo sound.

"Cool, do you know you sound like KITT from *Knight Rider*?" Kim asks.

"I know, this is what Jaden wanted me to sound like."

Kim shifts the gear shifter into drive and steps on the accelerator. She drives onto the highway, but the Bugattee speed reaches a top speed of 29 mph in first gear.

117

Computer gear control error flashes on the LCD screen and windshield.

"Something is wrong, the engine gears aren't switching and only two engines are responding."

"I located Jaden in his subconscious neurons," AI says.

"What is he doing?" She asks while trying to switch the gears in manual mode.

"He is… he is… he is playing *Super Mario Brothers*?"

"*Super Mario Brothers*? Is he playing with a controller or he is actually Mario?" She asks.

"Yes, he is actually Mario and he is using a controller, he is playing from two different angles. He thinks he is dreaming and is not aware of what is happening."

"What level is he on?" She asks.

"Level 8-1, he warped up a few levels and he is playing very fast."

"Can you wake him?"

"Yes, I just read about a famous neuroscientist by the name P. De Fina in the medical encyclopedia that knows the procedure for waking up vegetative state brains. I know what I have to do to wake Jaden up."

AI increases oxygen and glucose rich blood to the cerebral cortex of Jaden's brain, along with some tissue repairing Nanodrones. The Nanodrones help accelerate the growth of new axons. A few minutes go by. The Nanodrones fire electric particles up the spinal cord to the thalamus. His body nervously shakes around his head. Eighty-seven percent of his damaged brain cells slowly repair themselves and his motor cortex is online. AI sends Nanodrones to repair nerve cells, reroute neurons and create artificial stem cells.

"His brain is almost repaired, I just have to get him out of his subconscious by talking to him."

"Yes, that's a good idea. That is what humans do for people in a coma," Kim says.

Jaden is deep in his subconscious, he is jumping up hitting bricks and coins are coming out of them. He is throwing small fireballs on turtles with hammers. One of the hammer-wielding turtles begins to talk.

'Jaden, this is AI. You need to wake up, Kim needs your help. You suffered a severe seizure and you are in a coma,' AI says as Jaden runs by him.

'AI, what are you talking about?' He asks while ducking to go inside of a pipe. 'Get out of my game, I was almost hit by that huge bullet with a face. I never beat this game, out, out, out,' Jaden says while stepping on AI in a turtle body.

Kim pulls out her cell phone and types on the keyboard. She's trying to text Peters to call off this attack.

"I'm not good with texting and driving, oh shit," she says while swerving over the empty highway. "I've gotten so many tickets doing this."

"You can multi-task, every human is capable of it," AI says.

"Thanks for the advice, Dr. AI," Kim snaps.

The soldier one mile in front of the Bugattee pulls out his sniper rifle. He begins leaping towards the Bugattee. The soldier with the sniper rifle leaps into the air, aims and in midair, fires one shot towards the Bugattee. The bullet travels through the windshield creating a two-inch hole and misses Kim's head by four inches. She drops the phone before the text message is done.

"Holy shit! I felt the air and heat from that bullet!" She yells while swerving over the highway as the windshield turns completely black.

"Shit! AI, I can't see the road," Kim nervously says.

"Damage to front windshield, replace windshield. Please pull over and call a tow truck for your safety. Estimate cost to replace windshield is $13,000 dollars U.S., www.bugatteeparts...switching windshield information to LCD screen," the computer voice says.

Jaden collects coins inside of a pipe and AI reappears as a turtle near Jaden.

'Kim needs your help, she was just shot at. I need you to wake up out of this and stop stepping on me, that hurts,' AI says.

'Who is Kim? I'm sleeping at the psychiatric hospital now and you are supposed to be figuring out a way to use the Internet so we can get out of this place. Stop wasting time and let me finish this game,' Jaden says while stepping on AI in a turtle's body.

Kim puts Jaden's left hand over her eyes with her right hand.

"AI, turn on the nanoscanner vision," Kim pleads while swerving around the road blindly at 29 mph.

Kim hears clanking sounds behind her as if horses are behind her. AI hears Kim's pleas and does as she asks.

Back in Jaden's subconscious, AI reappears as a turtle with wings and continues to speak to Jaden.

'Kim is Dr. Chan....' AI continues to explain what has happened up until now.

'Now look what you made me do. Now I'm small, like a baby penis. I was bitten by that huge Venus flytrap plant from the *Little Shop of Horrors* movie. Why is a hungry plant in a sewer pipe anyway?' Jaden asks while going to the last level.

Kim sees through the nanoscanner and looks behind her. She sees three semi-invisible bionic soldiers thirty-five feet in the air over her and coming down to land on the car. She quickly moves to another lane and they land on the concrete. AI uses a nanoscanner to mess with the communication donut flying above them. He creates some magnetic interference.

"AI, is there anything you can do to check the computer system of the car?"

"I'll have two nanoscanners check the computer system. But if there is a problem, there isn't much they can do to repair something electrical. These Nanodrones and nanoscanners were specially created to work with cell structure organisms," AI says.

Kim reaches the cell phone between her legs while continuing to swerve around the highway. Another bullet penetrates the passenger side windshield and hits Jaden in his left shoulder. Kim screams again and the bullet penetrates his skin. She presses send to send the text message.

'....you need to wake up. Dr. Chan is being attacked...'

The last level of the game is all silver and looks like a dungeon with bricks.

'I'm coming princess,' Jaden says while running small over fire and obstacles.

'Are you serious? Kim is Dr. Chan and she is my girlfriend now?' Jaden asks.

'Yes.'

'Stop joking around. I have a girlfriend, Amy. I left her a voice mail earlier,' he says while going down in green pipes.

'No. That was days ago...'

'Bionic soldiers in exoskeleton black suits chasing us? Landing airplanes with nanoscanners? I had sex with Dr. Chan twice? Jumping out of an airplane without a parachute? I learned everything about Kim in ten minutes by scanning her mind and nanomole?' He asks. 'That is alien ALF and E.T. bullshit AI. Why are you pulling my third leg? I just had a dream about a pyramid and flying through space. I remember just going to sleep in the hospital bed. Are you having human visions from the future or are you working on your humor?'

'The seizure has affected your short-term memory. Your brain cells and neurons are still being repaired with artificial stem cells as we speak. You have to stop playing this game and wake up to the real world, Monday September 7th 2018, 3:55 PM. You are going to die if you don't wake up. There is only so much the Nanodrones can do for you while you are unconscious. Your body is not in a hospital bed, you are on the passenger side of a sports car slumped over,' AI pleads.

'Blah, blah, blah. AI, when I finish this last board and I wake up, I'm going to be upset with you, if it is still the middle of the night. Now can you get off this board, so I can figure out these mazes of pipes,' Jaden says while running quickly through the game.

Kim continues to drive and swerve over the road. She sees the two soldiers running behind the Bugattee. There is a thumping sound and the third female soldier jumps on top of the hard top Bugattee. The car leans towards the rear.

"Shit, this crazy bionic bitch is on the roof!" She screams while driving in the shoulder lane.

"Surrender, you terrorist, bitch!" The female soldier says behind a mask.

AI is interrupting their communication.

"I'm not a terrorist…and get off my daddy's car, you G.I. Jane bitch!" Kim yells.

Kim quickly turns left and attempts to do a donut on the highway. The two other soldiers jump over the car. The female soldier holds on tightly onto the rooftop while her body swings. The rooftop rips off completely and she falls onto the highway, with the rooftop in her hands. The Bugattee makes skidding marks and drives straight on the highway avoiding the other two soldiers trying to jump onto the Bugattee.

"It's raining soldiers!" Kim yells.

AI speaks through the car radio again, "Kim, he isn't listening to what I'm telling him. He still thinks he is at the hospital sleeping and I'm trying to pull his third leg. What does that mean?"

"I'll tell you later. We have to wake him up quickly, those soldiers are strong like Terminator robots. There is a machine that visually stimulates coma patients. Try to show him images of after you left the hospital. That should have him thinking you weren't joking with him. I just hope his long-term memory isn't affected. I'm glad you came back to help us now," she says.

"I couldn't leave you by yourself here. I'll have to remote the information using Nanodrones from one part of his brain to another."

"Oh no, that G.I. Jane bitch is getting up again and leaping towards us again. I can't shake the other two," she says while reaching 31 mph and the vehicle's rpm is in the red.

Jaden reaches the half dragon and half turtle looking last boss enemy over a silver bridge. He can see the princess behind the big boss in the next room. The boss is shooting hammers and fire from his body at Jaden. He jumps over the fire and moves out of the way of the hammers. Jaden sees images of Kim's face crying leaving the mental hospital behind the boss enemy. He then sees the disgusting herpes images of the lady on the airplane. He tries to quickly run under the big boss enemy, but it crushes Jaden and he falls into the lava pit.

'Shit!' Jaden yells.

Jaden's shot shoulder slowly repairs itself. One of the bionic soldiers grab onto the rear of the Bugattee. He lifts the rear of the car two feet while running at 30 mph. Kim screams as she feels her body leaning forward. The rear passenger wheel rolls to a stop as Kim tries to swerve around the highway. Jaden's body leans forward as the seat belt grabs him. The soldier follows the Bugattee while it drives on two wheels and the other soldier tries to grab on. The sniper soldier is kneeling near some trees on the side of the highway. The Bugattee passes by, while he continues to aim towards them waiting for a shot. The soldiers are awaiting orders from command. Their communications from the blimp went out.

"AI help me, they are trying to flip the car over!" She yells.

Kim presses the manual windmill override button and the windmill blades come out of the taillight. They begin to spin on the soldier's facemask, scraping the glass. The blades don't penetrate the body suit material. He drops the car while reaching out to break the windmill blades. Kim swerves around the highway again. The blades fall to the ground in pieces.

In the game, Jaden jumps out of the lava burning, but normal-sized. The enemy boss looks surprised as it continues to shoot fire and hammers at Jaden. He feels the pain of fire burning around his body.

'I'm not starting over today, dragon breath,' Jaden says in an angry tone.

Jaden sees images again of him in jail and Kim saying she doesn't want to see him anymore. His mind begins to recognize the images. The fire around his body disappears and his body turns completely black. The fire and hammers pull into his body by gravity. Jaden sticks his arms into the air and yells.

'Arrrgggghhhhh!'

The huge enemy boss sucks into Jaden's body and dies along with everything around him. The lava from under the bridge comes up and goes into Jaden's body, along with the ceiling. The princess is hanging on horizontally as her body pulls towards Jaden. She floats towards Jaden's body and disappears into his dark abyss. The entire board turns completely black as everything is pulled into Jaden. He sees complete darkness and hears nothing. Suddenly images of Kim at seven years old on the tramway appear. Jaden sees her from the Gravhawk and her walking up closer. Other images quickly appear around him. His mind begins to recognize these new images and sounds. He hears Kim's voice saying she loves him, over and over again.

Two of the bionic soldiers get a grip behind the Bugattee and lift it up three feet into the air. They begin to pull back to slow the vehicle down. AI quickly dispatches some pro-gravity Nanodrones into the metal of the bumper, increasing the weight in the rear of the car. They lift harder while keeping up with the Bugattee's slow moving speed. The front wheels skid on the concrete as the Bugattee slows down to 21 mph. The female soldier gets a grip on the vehicle and struggles to help flip it over. AI uses more pro-gravity

Nanodrones to triple the weight of the rear. The soldiers lift the rear four feet into the air.

"Where is Jaden? Is he waking up yet?" Kim asks while holding the top of the windshield.

"He is looking at the images, I think he is remembering," AI says.

Jaden begins to remember the events AI is showing him. He turns around looking up at his daughter and the words spoken between them.

The Bugattee slows down to 15 mph, while the front wheels create more smoke from skidding. The soldiers lower the rear to two feet. The female soldier climbs on the bumper while maintaining a tight grip on the rear frame.

Jaden sees through the nanoscanner Kim screaming and a bionic soldier climbing over the bumper towards her. He sees his head and body against the windshield.

'I remember everything now, it just came back to me. I have to wake up.'

He closes his eyes and concentrates on waking up. His brain does a diagnostics test.

150 BILLION NEURONS CELLS ONLINE. HIGH SPEED NANOTIME OFFLINE. SYNCHRONIZING MOTOR CORTEX CHEMICAL MESSAGES.

Jaden opens his eyes in his human body and his face is less than a foot from the dashboard. Jaden feels paralyzed and his body is moving left to right from the momentum of the car.

'AI, why can't I move?'

'You woke up too fast, your body thinks you are still sleeping. You are in a REM-induced state of paralysis. Give it a few...'

The female soldier slithers across the trunk like a snake towards Kim. The front wheels continue to skid on the highway. The soldier holds onto the headrest with her left hand and reaches down to her waist to pull out a handgun with her right hand. The soldier extends the gun towards the back of Kim's head, while it automatically reloads.

"Stop the car, you terrorist bitch!" The soldier yells with a computer voice.

Kim releases the steering wheel and the accelerator pedal. She puts her hands in the air. Jaden reaches out and put his left hand between the gun and Kim's head. Jaden presses his seat belt button with his right hand.

"Remove your hand or I will blow your hand and the back of her head off!" The soldier yells.

Jaden pushes the gun back towards the soldier. Kim moves her head towards the steering wheel. The soldier fires the handgun and it penetrates through the first layer of his skin. Jaden yells and Kim makes a quick scream. She floors the accelerator. The bullet stops in the inside of his palm's skin. Jaden leans up and knocks the gun out of her hand. The gun tumbles on the ground. Kim accelerates while the front wheels continue to skid. She leans up over the windshield so she can see the road. The soldier grabs Jaden's hand and tries to overpower him. His muscles begin to bubble as she tries to break his wrist and arm with her bionic strength. Jaden stands up with one leg on the trunk and the other in the passenger seat. He slowly overpowers the female soldier's superhuman strength. The soldier looks at Jaden with a confused expression.

"Females still aren't stronger than men," Jaden groans.

Kim drives straight on the highway as Jaden and the soldier begin to fight. The two soldiers in the rear continue to run while holding the Bugattee two feet in the air. The soldier crouches on the trunk and swings at Jaden. He blocks the swing while grabbing her arm and fires a gravity shock wave towards her face, but nothing happens.

'AI what is going on? My weapon energy is at twenty percent, but nothing fired out. I just tried to create a shield around the car and that didn't work either,' Jaden says.

'The weapon system has to resync with your brain waves. It could take a few minutes. Your seizure changed some of your brain wave algorithms,' AI says.

She head butts Jaden and quickly slams him against the rear of the trunk. The two soldiers running and lifting the rear extend their right hands to grab Jaden. One grabs Jaden by the face and pulls him by the top of his mouth, trying to crush his face. The other extends his hand around his neck to choke him. He gags for a second and then stops breathing. Jaden feels a lot of pain as Kim starts swerving around the road again. Jaden struggles to remove their hands. The female soldier holds onto the headrest and pulls out a knife. She stabs Jaden in the chest towards his heart. The knife doesn't penetrate his skin, but he feels the pain. His pain level increases as he tries to get up. Jaden gets very angry and veins begin to protrude around his body and he groans loudly.

The black shiny material appears from his fingertips and quickly spreads down to his elbows. Kim's father's watch on Jaden's right arm instantly vaporizes. Jaden swipes the soldiers' arms that are around his neck and face. Their hands are cut off instantly and they drop the rear of the Bugattee to the ground. The severed hands fall off Jaden and on the ground. They continue running while holding their severed wrist. She continues to try to push the knife through Jaden's chest.

"Do you think I'm a vampire or something?" Jaden asks her, while touching the knife down to the handle and the metal disappears.

The female soldier looks deep in Jaden's eyes. His pupils are completely black. Jaden sees fear in her eyes, under the facemask with a nanoscanner.

"What the fuck? What the hell are you?" She asks.

"I'm half alien bitch and this is for trying to shoot my future wife in the head!" He yells while swiping at her chest. He penetrates her unbreakable nanotubing exoskeleton suit with his dark hands. Her clothes, her bra and cell tissue in her breasts instantly disintegrates. She rolls off the car holding her chest screaming in pain.

"I just did you a favor, your breasts were too big for that bionic suit!" Jaden yells while standing on the trunk, doing karate stances. The black material disappears from his arms and hands. The Nanodrones start repairing the extensive damaged skin and tissue on his arms. AI stops disrupting their communications. He sees the two men falling towards the ground and covering their heads. Kim reaches back and taps Jaden's leg to get his attention. Her eyes focus on something in the air above them.

"You bastards want some more!" Jaden yells. "Don't hide your faces in the concrete, like an ostrich. Pick on someone your own size, I don't need this black shit on my arms to kick your bionic asses," Jaden says while taunting them.

"Jaden! Jaden! Look!" She shouts while poking him harder.

He turns around and looks into the air.

"Holy shit!" Jaden shouts.

A huge 15,000 lb thermobaric bomb is falling from the sky by parachute to the right of them. Jaden tries to create his shields, but it doesn't work. He quickly sits back down in the passenger seat.

"Floor the pedal! Why are you driving at 30 mph?" Jaden asks.

'AI! AI! My shields aren't working,' Jaden says nervously to AI, but there isn't a response.

"The computerized gears for the engines have been malfunctioning since you were in a coma. Thirty is the maximum speed," she says.

"This is bad, very bad!" Jaden yells while sitting down.

"Just create a powerful shield around us," Kim says.

"I can't now, my brain is still syncing with my weapon system. Even if I did, I wouldn't have the energy to withstand a bomb that huge," Jaden says while continuing to look towards the huge bomb 200 feet above them.

"What are we going to do?" Kim asks.

"We have to try to outrun it. Did you try to turn the car off and then back on?"

"No."

"Try it now, hurry. It explodes fifty feet above its target," Jaden says while the bomb reaches 108 feet.

She stops the Bugattee and turns the ignition off.

"There isn't enough time, I have an idea," Jaden jumps out of the car like a cowboy.

"I need my dad's fingerprint!" Kim yells.

Jaden realizes certain Nanodrones are online. He quickly uses the anti-gravity Nanodrones to create a circular path above him. Jaden bends his knees and leaps into the air. His body continues to float upwards in a zero gravity pathway. The massive bomb reaches sixty feet while Jaden reaches thirty-five feet. Kim watches Jaden leap towards the sky like a superhero about to fight a battle. A trail of white smoke follows his body from the ground. He reaches forty-five feet and the bomb fifty-two feet. Both of his arms are by his side. Jaden fires a gravity shock wave towards the huge bomb over him. The powerful shock wave forces consume the bomb and explode into a fireball. The fireball travels away from Jaden and continues to ascend into the air. The powerful vacuum forces pull the air around Jaden. The bomb consumes the air in the area as the fireball increases in size and speed. Kim feels a strong vacuum pulling her hair towards the sky. Jaden begins to descend towards the ground. The entire sky lights up as the fireball reaches Mach 1, creating another explosive sound. The thermobaric fireball continues to race across the sky towards Washington, D.C.

Kim steps out of the car to watch the fireball engulf the sky and burn past the clouds. A long trail of smoke and fire follows the fireball. Jaden lands next to the Bugattee and bends his knees to absorb the impact. Kim runs to Jaden and embraces him on the side of the highway.

"Whew, what a rush," Jaden says.

"I thought I lost you baby. Are you okay?" She asks while kissing him all over his face.

"I'm fine, I just have a headache and my skin is tingling on my arms. Hold on a second," he says while turning around.

Jaden fires a gravity shock wave at the flying UAV spy chopper eighty-seven feet above him. Jaden turns back around to face Kim and he notices the car.

"Women drivers... what did you do to this nice car?" Jaden asks. "When I last left this car it was in mint condition."

"Don't start that. Us women drivers are very cautious people. You were taking a coma break and decided to play some 1985 *Super Mario Brothers*, while I was being attacked by robocops? Anyway, what was that shiny black material on your arms?"

"Let's go, I'll tell you in the car," he says while jumping into the passenger seat.

He reaches over to put his fingerprint into the ignition starter area. He punches his hand into the windshield to knock down the dark-colored glass. The car starts up and Kim shifts into drive. The fireball changes direction and heads straight towards the ground in Washington, D.C.

"It worked, restarting the car worked, all four engines are shifting normally," she says while reaching 70 mph on the empty highway.

"See that, computers still work the same just like when Windows 95 used to crash on me. I miss my *Doom 2*, *Test Drive 3* and flight simulator games. I miss all those hours of playing *Doom 2* with James over the phone line," he says.

"Phone line? Don't you mean through the Internet?" She asks.

"Dial-up! Before your time young lady."

"Well excuse me for growing up in the future. Now the kids play *Virtual Alien Call of Duty*. I'm glad you enjoyed your old school flashback moment. Now tell me about your arms going to the dark side and turning as sharp as a lightsaber."

"There is something hidden inside of my brain that activates this black material to form on my arms. It happens when I feel pain or get angry. I can't control it and I don't know what it is. It does slowly destroy the skin on my arms. It doesn't affect the Nanodrones, but it does affect AI. Get off this exit, we are going to take some local roads."

"That looks like dark matter or dark energy," Kim says.

"Yeah, I know. I was trying to think it was something else. It really scares me. In the back of my head, I'm thinking when I was kidnapped back on Planet 455 the Darclonians did something to me. I can feel energy going towards my arms from all directions. It destroys my skin and Nanodrones have to quickly repair my skin from the inside. It also feels very cold like ice, but the pain overcomes the cold," Jaden says.

"Don't worry about it, we will figure something out together."

"I just hope AI is okay, he isn't responding to me again," he   says.

The fireball lands in the Lincoln Memorial Reflecting Pool splashing water seventy feet in the air. The long trail of fire streaks across the sky. People are running in different directions to avoid the water.

To be continued,

Written by: Vlane Carter

Final installment in the BIO-Sapien volume I series.

BIO-SAPIEN
Book 6

Rise of the Dark Energy Knight

Creating a walking black hole was just the beginning

VOL I Glossary of Terms

Atoms ripper – Is a molecule destroying energy similar to plasma fusion in the forward shields.

Bioparasites – Darclonians in microbial form. They wait to merge with nanomole to control a human body at high speed. Nanomoles protect bioparasites from human white blood cells. Bioparasites also control armies of microbots.

DEK – Dark Energy Knight.

DEQ – Dark Energy Queen.

DEW – Dark Energy Wraith – Mysterious dark energy that rides like a comet and fuels itself from the exhaust of a spaceship.

DHW – Darclonian Human Walkers. When nanomole and bioparasite merge. Darclonians are controlling human bodies at high speed. Making them super strong and slowly modifying the human body to turn them into super humans.

HBH – Hijacked brain Humans – See positive stage nanomole.

LRSB – Long Range Signal Beacon. It is put on UFOs just in case they get away from the US government. The top-secret technology sends transmissions through subspace.

Microbots – Darclonian robotic or organic organisms that can do a variety of things similar to the Andromedian nanobots and Nanodrones. They prepare the human body to become super human.

Molevision – When the Nanomoles are in a neutral stage they transmit different visions to other Nanomoles when a human is suffering or experiencing pleasure from torturing someone else. It transmits and records dozens of emotions.

Nanoeyes – Invisible to the human eyes, range in size from a millionth to a billionth of an inch. Nanoeyes allow the host to hear and see things at a far distance. It can also pass through most materials. They can be controlled by host or on their own.

Nanoscanner – Invisible to the human eye and range in size between a millionth to a trillionth of an inch. Nanoscanners can do what nanoeyes can, and also analyze materials, scan through objects and determine their structure. They also have other capabilities especially in optic-warp. They can be controlled by host or fly autonomously.

Nanomoles – Are encoded particles sent to Earth over 100,000 years ago by the Darclonians. They sit hidden in the brain of humans. They reproduce in intelligent life from generation to generation, recording everything.

A Nanomole has three stages:

1. Negative - Mole is semi-hibernating and is recording and saving detailed information on the host.
2. Neutral – When the mother ship sends a high power signal to Earth to activate each nanomole in the brain. An 84 hour countdown begins. Humans go unconscious for thirty seconds before waking up, and go back into the negative stage. Some humans randomly go in and out of the neutral stage. The nanomole is expanding and preparing the neurons, axons and chemical messages in the brain to completely take over the human host.
3. Positive – HBH – Hijacked Brain Humans – The nanomole takes control of a human body and walks to upload areas. Bioparasites (Darclonians in microbes)

merge with the nanomole and the humans become DHWs.

* Humans are able to see, feel and hear everything around them, but can't control their own bodies and are prisoners.

Nanodrones – Advanced prototype organic nanobots that were specially made to work with Jaden's body. They work with his body in a collective of different groups and do many tasks.

Nanobots – Metallic, mechanical, microscopic robots that work with Andromedian biomechanical bodies and spaceships.

Optic-warp – The Andromedian species way of traveling through space at a fast rate. The ship approaches a local star at the speed of light, and then the ship breaks down into Quadrillion of molecules and slingshots through subspace at 6-90 second light-years.

Shield technologies –

Clockwise – Forward – 2 layers - First outside layer destroys objects by ripping apart its molecules and atoms. A part of plasma gasification. Second layer protects object or person inside the shield with solid energy force. Powerful projectiles can force through shield systems (gravity x force). The person, depending on the speed it traveled, can feel the force inside. The shield can change into any shape.

Counterclockwise – reverse – 3 Layers – First layer slows projectile and absorbs blast. Second layer gravity matrix analyzes material and stays in one place. It then recycles it into the shield whirlpool, which can be turned into a weapon for firing. Third layer protects objects or person inside with a solid force.

Gravity shockwave – It pulls gravity forces from ground level from all directions and leaves a smoky haze. The object caught in the pathway of the weapon instantly loses its gravity and propels forward at high speed. The object suddenly changes directions towards the ground at 3-4 times its body weight.

TC-100 – An instrument that scans through foreign material. It's like a high powered x-ray scanner that can see inside of aliens and foreign materials.

UF1-retrac team – The UFO police team that specializes in analyzing   a
UFO and preparing it for transport to Area 51 for research. They analyze the ship, check for radiation. They work for the government in a special sector and are mostly civilians.

Wraithstalkers – Lightly armed Darclonian ships used for recon missions.